COMING HOME

JENNIFER LYNN

SOUL SONG PRESS, LLC

Published by Soul Song Press, LLC.

www.SoulSongPress.com

ISBN 979-8-9897418-0-9 (Paperback)

ISBN 979-8-9897418-1-6 (Ebook)

*For the Goddess, the Great Mother, and
Her song of peaceful loving.*

AUTHOR'S NOTE

Welcome to *Coming Home*!

Throughout Bree MacLeod's story, you will encounter words, phrases and concepts from the Celtic mystical, druidic, and shamanic traditions. To preserve their integrity and authenticity, these ideas are often presented in their source language, primarily Gaelic.

No doubt many of you may be unfamiliar with this ancient tongue. No worries. To help you identify any such words and more easily connect with their magic and mystery, Gaelic words appear in italics throughout the story. While explanations are provided both through the narrative and context, a more complete glossary of these terms is included at the back of this book. Beyond the glossary is a list of references and resources, for those inspired to seek the Truth at the root of Bree's fiction.

May the light of *Imbas* ever flame the fire in your head.

Beannachtaí... Blessings.

Jennifer Lynn

1

Cold. Bree MacLeod closed her eyes and shivered. Wrapping her arms around her torso, she bent over her folded legs and drew herself closer to the earth of the grove in search of warmth. She found only cold.

Ghostly, ice-covered fingers reached through her black fleece and pierced the cotton sleeves beneath before raking her skin and bones. Bree's body shook, rattling the Otherworldly tentacles. With a thud, the edges cracked under the sheer. Flakes of ice cascaded like endless snows falling deeper toward her core, but the Fomorian grip held.

No wonder the Norsemen feared the Frost Giants. The thought raced through her unbidden. Bree grimaced, unable to push through the drifts for a full smile. Was that humor? At a time like this?

"Focus, chiya." A voice—feminine, ancient, loving—rippled through her from the Otherworld.

Bree opened her eyes to darkness. Around her, the trees of the grove stood watching, waiting. She knew they were there, encircling her, even if the darkness hid them from her. She remembered walking through their twining embrace to enter the grove earlier that night.

So peaceful, the trees had welcomed her, had wrapped her in their ancient whispering. Now they stood silent, muted. That song and its healing power were lost to her, veiled beyond the crushing cold. She could not reach for that vibration, could not draw it into her nor send it rushing through her to unleash her inner fire. She had tried. Instead, the Otherworldly fist had gripped her, smothering her in darkness and ice.

Cold. Bree shivered and turned her head toward the sky.

Darkness stared back at her. A few stars smoldered in the distance, frozen pinpricks of light too remote and obscure to bother with her. She could reach forever and never touch their light. And the cold would take her.

Even her trusted friend the Moon hid from her, veiled in Night's blanket. Bree's eyes tracked a shadow as it branched through the deepening dark. She watched it curl into eyelashes resting upon an ancient cheek curving through the sky.

The eye of the Goddess, Bree thought. But that eye remained closed in Her monthly rest, Her light shuttered even to Bree.

Still, she knew the Goddess was watching. Her presence, vast and ancient, leaned upon the edges of Bree's awareness, like the weight of the ocean pressing eternally upon the sea floor. She, too, was waiting.

Waiting for what? Bree wondered.

What was it her Teacher, the goddess Bríghid had said when Bree entered the grove tonight? She shivered, casting her consciousness back, searching through the cold to the moment before everything went dark. Bríghid's voice—feminine, ancient, loving—washed anew through Bree, this time bathed with the voice of the Goddess.

"It is time. You must kindle your own fire and claim your light, or slumber forever in darkness."

Bríghid and the Goddess had brought her to the grove this night. Bree could feel the Truth of intention aching in her bones. She knew They were watching and waiting for her to choose. But, choose what?

How could she choose when she didn't understand the question?

Icy fingers bored deeper into her, cold seeping to her bones. Bree gasped as an image flashed through her inner vision. Somewhere in the darkness of the Otherworld, Fomorian eyes—glittering, harsh and perishing—leered.

Bree shook. Dropping her head, her nose rubbed against the earth.

Fire. She needed heat to disperse the thickening freeze. How to kindle it? The trees and the Moon had always been there for her. They had always offered their light and life force to support her. Until now. Why? What had changed? What were her Allies trying to teach her? Here, now, what was she supposed to do?

Bree shivered in the darkness. With a sigh, she rested her forehead upon the earth. "What did Bríghid say earlier? 'Kindle your own fire.' But how?"

The earth rumbled beneath Bree. Power shifted and pulsed, rushing upward and spilling to encompass her in a slowly widening circle. With each gush, the icy grip slackened around her until a hint of warmth crept in, flowing along her bones and easing the pain. A voice—fertile, lyrical and vast—rose from the earth and filled the circle.

"To kindle your own flame, you must first know who you are."

Eyes, swirling with the browns of rich, loamy soil and the greens of the forest, opened and filled Bree's awareness. Her heart pounded. To Bree's surprise, another heartbeat sang back to her, rising with the rumbling energy and pulsing with the earth below.

"Earth Mother?" Bree whispered, her breath misting dew upon the grass.

A smile flashed, spilling warmth through Bree.

She gasped as the icy tendrils quivered, inching back toward the surface. She knew it was only a reprieve. The challenge was not yet complete and that Fomorian grip still held her. But she was so grateful. Tears flooded her eyes.

The resonant voice of the Earth Mother rippled up and through her again. *"Who are you?"*

Bree shivered, as much from the cold as from uncertainty. She had experienced enough in twenty years of training with Mother Bríghid to recognize an initiation in progress. They were never as straightforward as they seemed. And this time, Bree was, quite literally, in the dark from the beginning.

Who am I? She considered the question as her body shivered. *Could it be that simple? Could that really be the answer?*

"The only way forward is through..." It was one of her Salmon Ally's favorite sayings. Although Salmon's voice had not penetrated to find her here, Bree smiled. The memory was reassuring enough to encourage her.

Pressing her forehead gently upon the grass of the grove, Bree spoke directly to the Earth Mother. "I am Bree MacLeod."

Bree's world shook. Her body trembled as the earth below her rumbled and quaked. Ice poured through her, gripping her tighter and dispelling all warmth. With a shudder, she cried out.

"I don't understand!"

Loamy green eyes rushed toward her. Rising out of the earth, they stopped at the end of her nose and glared as a voice screamed through her soul.

"You bring that name here?"

The earth shook violently beneath her, and Bree dropped frozen hands to the ground in an effort to steady herself. Cold fire speared up her hands and arms, and she gasped.

"I don't understand! It is the name I was given! How did I offend?"

"You come here, to the sacred grove, to the enclosure blessed of the Goddess. You, the daughter of the goddess Bríghid, the first-born of Her sacred line, blessed in Her earth, Her water, Her flame. Yet, here, in this space of the Mother, you deign to clothe yourself in the name of the father?"

The earth shook, tossing Bree violently. Each bump seared through her frozen body. She dug frigid fingers into the ground, creating handholds to stop herself from tumbling.

"True, his blood has merit, married as it is to the Ancient Race and flowing with the sacred blood of the Sídhe. This was why the bonding was allowed." The glowering eyes narrowed before Bree, then drew back toward the earth. *"Tell me, Daughter of the Chalice... Is this the name you choose?"*

Bree trembled. The earth beneath her stilled and a hush

settled around her. Cold still encased her and pierced, rigid as steel, where the icicles penetrated her. The fingers of that Fomorian fist hovered all around her, muscles twitching, waiting to clasp onto her for good.

Go carefully, she cautioned herself. *Think well before you speak next.*

She held no ill will toward her father or the name his clan gifted her. She would not have discarded or deemed it improper in any way. Quite the opposite. She had always been proud of her clan and its connection to the *Sídhe*. But, shivering in the darkness, she wondered for the first time—is there more? Did the name Bree MacLeod limit her in some way? Was she other than Bree MacLeod?

"Who are you?"

The voice of the Earth Mother pounded through Bree. As icy fingers gripped more tightly, she crumpled onto the ground. Panting shallowly, her voice was a whisper upon the earth.

"I don't know."

Images flooded through her, releasing ghostly voices from her past. "Raven Child! Raven Child!" The words rang sing-song from her six-year-old self. The circle of children had spat their taunt for her coloring and Irish blood.

Could they have known they spoke the Truth? Bree still wondered.

The words of the taunt blurred, sliding and stretching in pitch until the voice of Emily, Bree's aunt and foster-mother, rang through her. "You are a *Bean feasa*, a wise woman, a druid. One of the *Aes Dána*, the Gifted who can see and move through the Veil..."

Emily! Bree cried mentally, hoping her aunt might hear. But memory dragged her onward.

"Crrruck!"

The call of her Raven Ally echoed and rippled, birthing the voice of her dead mother, Bríde. "The women of our bloodline are the daughters of Bríghid, the Celtic goddess of the Sacred Flame. It is Her blood that gifts you, that calls your soul to the Work. While Her blood flows through us all, only the first-born daughter carries the fullness of Her Gift."

Black and glistening, Raven's eye stared to her depths, as her mother's voice resounded. "Bree, you are the first-born daughter...."

Sinking into Raven's eye, blackness engulfed her. Bree shivered, the vision pulling her deeper. Golden light etched a circle that pulsated and beamed, morphing outward until Bree saw herself standing before Bríghid. The goddess smiled, releasing rays of light to stream around Bree.

Touching her forehead, the goddess whispered, *"Beannachtaí, mo Ghrá... Blessings, my Love."*

Bree shook her head, her forehead pressing upon the earth. "But which one? Which one am I? Which of these is Truth?"

"Truth has many facets," the voice of Bríghid echoed through her awareness.

"And many faces," the Earth Mother added. *"All of which are true."*

Warmth flashed in Bree's core. Heat radiated, driving the icicles outward and forcing the icy grip to slacken.

"Who are you?" The Earth Mother demanded anew.

Bree lay crumpled upon the ground. Her feet and fingers were numb beyond feeling and her body trembled in the cold. But inside, something sparked, promising a fire. She closed her eyes, listened to that sizzle, then spoke once more to the earth.

"I am Bree—*Bean feasa*, Raven Child, and the first-born Daughter of the goddess Bríghid."

Heat blazed, searing outward from the center of her to fill her entire being. A shrill whine screamed from the Otherworld, then faded as the last of the icicles melted and sputtered in the flame.

The Fomorian fist jerked free of her, rocking Bree onto her back. Eyes still closed, she watched with her inner vision as light poured through her, flooding from her soul to her body and her energy field.

Fire rushed and something touched her forehead. A pressure filled her awareness as a pinpoint of golden radiance blazed to life above the inner corner of her left eyebrow. Sliding to the right, the light arched downward, passed just above the bridge of her nose, and curved back upward to hover above the inner corner of her right eyebrow. With a flash, it arched slowly downward again, this time passing well above the bridge of her nose as it seared a line on its way toward her left eyebrow. The image of a crescent flamed through Bree's inner vision.

"The Eye of the Goddess is now open." Bríghid's voice rang through her. *"In the grove She awaits you. Walk forever in Her Love."*

Lips pressed against Bree's newly-blessed brow and light flooded as a vast eye slid open within her. The earth solid and reassuring beneath her back, Bree opened her physical eyes and blinked back tears. Above her, a single line of silvery light curved as the eye of the Goddess, newly awakened, spilled a shaft of moonlight, soft and luminous, upon Bree and the grove.

"Welcome, Bree Nic Bhríde, the Love of Bríghid," the crescent moon greeted her.

Bree choked out a sob as her hands, now blazing hot, pressed lovingly upon the earth. A breeze drifted over her, carrying the tender song of the trees.

"Welcome, Bree Nic Bhríde," they sang. *"Welcome, the Love of Bríghid."*

Bree lifted a trembling hand and touched her aching forehead. A thin line burned under her fingers as she followed the mark along its arching path. With a gasp, she sat up and found herself staring into the loving gaze of Mother Bríghid.

Heat seared anew across Bree's forehead as the goddess gathered her trembling hands into Her own.

"Welcome, Bree Nic Bhríde, mo Ghrá... my Love."

2

Bree opened her eyes to brilliance. Sunlight streamed, soft and welcoming, through the windows of her bedroom. Birdsong drifted through the thatching of her cottage as the cows in the neighboring pasture lowed, and she smiled.

She loved waking to the song of life in the Kildare countryside. Her little thatched cottage, inherited upon her mother's death, had proven to be her refuge, especially over the past year. Here the noise of This World fell away, gifting Bree true relief.

Nestled at the heart of Bríghid's home county, Bree sensed the Love of the mother of her lineage pulsing through her with each step upon that sacred earth. At night, she could hear the Mother of Ireland, blessed Éireann singing her to sleep. Of all the places she had called home—Seattle, Cape Breton, Saint Louis, Ireland —here, more than anywhere else, she lived knowing herself sheltered in the palm of the Goddess.

Bree could still remember the first time her feet had touched the *machair*, the soil of Éireann's Blessed Isle. Breaking free of the din of Dublin, Bree had stripped off her shoes and walked barefoot upon Mother Éireann.

"I am here," Bree had whispered.

The response had flowed gently, a loving embrace that

enfolded Bree from her feet to her head, then draped gently around her shoulders. Wrapped in Éireann's blessing, all the noise simply quieted. The aching, the yearning that pursued and haunted Bree throughout this lifetime had simply vanished.

Bathed in peace, Bree had heard Mother Éireann whisper...

"...*Fáilte abhaile... Welcome home.*"

Bree snuggled deeper into her blankets, pulling them under her chin. Yes, she loved her little Irish cottage, as much as—if not more than—her mother had. The call of the cows rumbled, soft and soothing, washing through Bree like the heartbeat of the earth, and she smiled.

"Good morning," she whispered, then rolled onto her side.

Pain seared through her head. Shifting quickly onto her back, Bree groaned. Instinctively, she reached and pressed a palm against her throbbing forehead, then gasped. Fire blazed as her fingers tracked the thin welt upon her brow.

Bree closed her eyes and dropped her hand to the mattress. *It is real. I did not dream it.*

"*It will burn until you embrace it fully.*"

Bree opened her eyes and sat up to find herself held in the tender gaze of Mother Bríghid.

"*And yes, it will be visible in This World and the Otherworld, to those with eyes to see.*"

Bree blinked. "You mean, others will be able to see it?"

Mother Bríghid smiled softly, and fire blazed across Bree's forehead.

Inside her a spark caught and flared to a flame. Some corner of her mind whispered something about questions, but she could not focus through the rush to hear it clearly. Heat scorched, bellowing from her depths and belching rage to roast her being. Bree seethed. She opened her mouth to speak, then closed it.

Bríghid's head tilted. "*What is it, my Love?*"

Bree dropped her gaze to the bed and shook her head. She would not speak words of wrath to her Teacher.

Cooling tenderness cascaded down the left side of Bree, and she watched from the corner of her eyes as Bríghid stroked her hair.

Bree stiffened. The energetic contact, she knew, would transmit her turmoil. It would be as if she had shouted her rage directly into her Teacher's face. Inhaling, Bree drew her energy field tighter around her and sealed it, shielding herself from the touch of the goddess.

She saw Bríghid flinch and withdraw her hand quickly. Light crackled and hissed along the edges of Bree as the goddess scanned her energetic field.

"You are angry," Bríghid frowned. *"Why, my Love?"*

Bree sighed. There was no hiding it. The goddess would see it one way or another. Bracing herself to moderate the fiery rush spewing inside her, she lifted her gaze.

"My name." She stared at Bríghid, anger flashing through her to spark along the edges of her energetic body. "In my twenty-eight years I've lost my home, my family, even my beloved. Now, you take my name. Why?"

A smile spread tenderly across Bríghid's face. *"To reveal your true name."*

Not good enough, Bree seethed. She sat and stared at her Teacher, rage glaring.

Bríghid's face softened. *"To call you home to the Truth of yourself."*

Bree dropped her gaze, unwilling to argue further with the Mother of her lineage. Bree trusted Bríghid. She knew the goddess cared for her and, thus far, had always guided her lovingly. But, to take her *name*. She clenched her fists.

It is all I have left.

Rage flared inside Bree and she shook. MacLeod was a good name, an old name, one flowing with the blood of the People of Peace, the Shining Ones, *the Sídhe*. She was proud of her Scottish ancestry, had marched every summer in Cape Breton with her kin in the annual parade of clans. Wearing the green and purple hunting plaid of the MacLeods of Skye, Bree came the closest to feeling like she belonged.

"It was good enough for my birth."

Her voice pitched low, Bree spoke the words before she could stop them. To her inner eye, the words hung there, shimmering in the air between her and the goddess, shaking with unspoken challenge.

Golden light flashed across Bree as Bríghid stiffened.

"True. Good it was for your birth and for the years before your initiation."

Light pulsed around Bree, sparkling and glinting as if reflecting off metal. Pressure rippled along Bree's awareness, tracing from her head to her feet, then Bríghid sat back and nodded.

"Perhaps it is time for you to remember your true connection to the name."

Bree lifted her gaze to meet the eyes of the goddess as the bouncing notes of an Irish jig rang out from her telephone. The dance of sound echoed off the stone walls of her cottage, spilling from the kitchen through to her bedroom.

"Answer the call, chiya," Bríghid smiled. *"Accept the invitation and discover the Truth hidden within you."*

Bree frowned. "I don't understand..."

The jig reeled anew and Bree turned toward the sound.

"Answer it, my Love."

Bríghid's voice washed through Bree. She turned back, mouth open to speak, but the goddess was gone.

3

Bree threw back the flannel sheets and gasped as her bare feet touched the chilly tile floor. Rising to her toes, she scampered out of her bedroom and through the dining nook. Reaching across the kitchen counter, she grabbed her telephone.

"+01470?" Bree wondered aloud, reading the area code that flashed on the display.

Bríghid's voice washed again through her. *"Answer the call and discover the Truth."*

Okay, Bree thought as she unplugged the telephone from its charger. Touching answer on the screen, she lifted the telephone to her ear.

"Hello?"

"Bree?" A female voice greeted her. "Raven Child, is that you?"

The voice was familiar. Strong, it echoed with laughter and just a hint of Scottish brogue. She was certain she had heard the voice before. Bree furrowed her brow.

"This is Bree MacLeod."

"Bríghid be praised! I cannae believe I actually reached ye! Thought for certain to be speaking with an answering service again. Ach, blessed Rose! She promised this number would ring true."

Now instinct, her training engaged and Bree sank into the voice. Vision blurred as her energy field pulsated, instinctively seeking resonance with the vibration of the caller. Geometric shapes filled her awareness as they popped into and out of focus, dancing with the lilt of the woman's voice. Bree watched as three triangles etched themselves to overlap at thirty-degree angles. White light blazed, tracking their edges then illuminating the whole.

In that flash Bree was a girl again, running barefoot across the sand two steps behind red-haired pigtails. Arms bared to the summer sun, she and the girl plunged toward the sea, laughing. The waters rose over her, throwing Bree into a night sky. She shivered and sank deeper into her tartan wrap as a bonfire blazed. Somewhere nearby bagpipes wailed a dirge. An arm enfolded her and Bree turned to see tears washing a young face enfolded in red hair. Firelight blazed and that same face, now a teenager, smiled back at Bree.

No, it can't be. Bree thought. *The area code for Cape Breton is 902.*

The image of the red-headed girl laughed in Bree's awareness as earth-colored eyes winked. Bree inhaled deeply, shifting her vision back to This World as she spoke.

"Caitlin?"

4

"I heard ye were in Ireland, moping."

A smile radiated to Bree through the telephone. She chuckled and shook her head. Sleep-tossed black hair danced loose around her face and shoulders.

"Grieving. The correct term is grieving."

"Mmmm-hm. If ye say so." Laughter echoed through Bree's awareness, flowing in her kinswoman's voice. "Well, how about a change of scenery, then?"

Caitlìn MacLeod.

They had been summer friends, running wild together under the Cape Breton sky. Kinswomen, they shared the name MacLeod but had no direct blood relation, despite their best efforts to create one. Caitlìn's mother was born MacLeod of Skye, and her father MacLeod of Cape Breton. A kinsman to Bree's father, the two men were likely distant relatives, but the connection was lost to the past.

"Well, we can choose to be sisters and no one can tell us otherwise." Caitlìn's voice drifted out of Bree's memory and she smiled. She could still see her young friend, face set in fierce determination, grabbing Bree's hand and refusing to let go.

Bree pursed her lips. She remembered those early summers alone.

A true child of Nova Scotia, her father had insisted on returning to his home to spend the summers with his family there. How he arranged it with his Seattle boss, to this day Bree could not imagine. But arrange it he did, and Bree spent three months each year as a guest amongst her father's people and ignored by the local children.

Until Caitlìn walked up to Bree and declared them best friends. From that moment on, Caitlìn had dragged Bree everywhere and had dared the other kids to refuse.

She was always looking after me, Bree smiled, remembering.

The sound of bagpipes wailing a dirge echoed as the arm of her friend reached from the past to press anew across Bree's shoulders. Caitlìn's touch was the only warmth she had known on that horrible night. The eve of her ninth birthday. Bree had shivered with Otherworldly cold throughout the funeral service, despite her tartan wrap and the flickering bonfire. Choosing to remain with his kin in Nova Scotia, her father insisted on burying her mother's ashes in Cape Breton, so he could "have her near." Bree often wondered if he buried something of himself with his wife. He certainly had no comfort for anyone that night or any time thereafter.

Caitlìn was Bree's constant companion that night and for the next two years, until Bree was sent to live with her aunt Emily and cousin Rose in Seattle. With her father lost in his grief, Caitlìn's mother quietly took care of Bree, welcoming her into both home and family. She and Caitlìn had shared a bedroom then and, in their own way, finally became sisters.

When Bree fled Seattle for a new home and a new life, Caitlìn celebrated Bree's search for a place to belong. But the violence of Bree's departure had left Bree shaken and introverted. Instead of thriving at Washington University, Bree found herself withdrawing, unwilling to risk similar rejection. She still remembered sobbing her misery one afternoon to Caitlìn over the telephone. The next morning, Bree woke to the sound of pounding on her dorm room door. When she opened it, Caitlìn had pushed past her, dumped her bag on Bree's bed and declared, "This weekend we make you some friends."

One year older than her, Caitlìn was as much a sister to Bree as Rose was. Bree and Caitlìn had remained close, even as life carried them in different directions. Bree discovered a new life for herself in Saint Louis, while Caitlìn completed her studies at Trent University in Ontario and returned home to Cape Breton. Years could pass without contact, but they always managed to find each other in times of transition or need.

Just like Caitlìn to turn up now.

Bree gasped quietly. She lifted her hand toward her aching forehead, then stopped and let it fall. *Of course Brìghid would call her to me now.*

"How say ye, Raven Child? Are ye up for it?"

Bree's forehead pulsed. "What exactly do you mean—'A change of scenery'?"

"Well," Caitlìn's voice sparkled with laughter through the telephone. "Ye can *'grieve'* in Scotland as well as ye can in Ireland."

Bree stifled a chuckle. Leave it to Caitlìn to make quotation marks audible in spoken conversation.

"And why would I go to Scotland when I am quite comfortable in Ireland?"

"Grrummmph. To see me, of course!"

Bree let herself laugh. Warmth coursed from her heart to her limbs, bathing bone and muscle in shimmering radiance along the way. As tension spilled out of her, Bree grinned.

It felt good to laugh. Come to think of it, it felt good just to smile. She really had not been doing much of either lately, not since she left her cousin Rose's house three months ago. Bree knew it was time to start living again. Gwen's visit from the Otherworld had made that perfectly clear. But, Bree could not figure out how.

A voice whispered in the back of her mind, *There is more.*

Bree cleared her throat. "Well, that is one reason, certainly. But, if you're worried about me..."

"Too right, I'm worried about ye." Caitlìn's voice broke in. "Gwen *died*—a year ago—and ye did nay even call me."

Bree slumped, leaning back against the kitchen counter. *One year, three months and nine days.*

The hurt in her friend's honest reply ached along her bones. Silence stretched, begging Bree to offer some kind of explanation. Her lips moved, searching for the words and finding none. *What can I say?*

Caitlìn cleared her throat. "But... well... truth is—I need your help."

"My help?"

"Aye." A sigh spilled through the telephone, bathing Bree in sorrow. "Alistair died."

Images of a tall, broad-shouldered man with dark, bristling hair and sad, grey eyes raced through Bree. Alistair was the brother of Caitlìn's father, and he had lived with the family in Cape Breton for a while when she and Caitlìn were young. Bree could still hear his deep belly-laugh and taste the sweets he smuggled to them, much to the disapproval of Caitlìn's mother. Once, at the shore, Bree ran herself to exhaustion chasing the waves as she searched for undines. Unable to walk back to camp, Alistair had lifted her onto his shoulders and carried her.

Tears welled in Bree's eyes. "Oh, Caitlìn, I am so sorry."

"Aye."

Tension thrummed in her friend's voice. The sound trembled through Bree's memory, shaking loose words from another conversation.

"I never told her I was sorry."

Only three years ago Caitlìn's mother died. Bree had listened to her friend weeping through the telephone and tried to ease her despair. The next day, Bree kissed Gwen goodbye and caught the first flight out of Saint Louis with a connection to Halifax, bags packed to stay for a month. During the services, Bree remained at her friend's side, her arm ever ready to enfold grieving shoulders in support. Afterwards, Bree had held Caitlìn, rocking her friend while the girl cried until she could cry no more.

Just as she did for me.

"Would you like me to come with you?" Bree found her own voice heavy.

"That's kind of ye, truly," Caitlìn began. "But, no. Actually, I need you to look after the B&B for me, while I am away. 'Tis finally running brilliantly, and I cannae close it on such short notice. It'd cost me dear."

"Heather House..." Bree nodded. "I'd forgotten."

"Will ye come, then?"

"Accept the invitation and discover the Truth hidden within you." As Brìghid's voice washed through her, Bree shivered.

"Sure." Bree sighed, touching her forehead gingerly. "Sure, I'll come."

5

"How long will you be in Scotland?"

Bree sat on the bed in her cottage. An open suitcase rested, half full, beside her. She pulled restlessly at a pair of wool socks waiting to be packed.

"Bree? Did I lose you?" Fergus Sinclair called through the telephone.

Bree sighed. "No, I'm still here."

"How long will you be in Scotland?" Fergus asked again.

Bree could hear the yearning in his voice. It ached, pulsing through her like a heartbeat.

"I don't know exactly."

She was avoiding him and she knew it.

They had been friends for several years and had grown quite close over the last three. Fergus was kind, supportive and encouraging, always offering a laugh when Bree needed it most.

A year ago, when Gwen passed and Bree fell to pieces, Fergus had been there for her. He had brought food and sat with her, making sure she ate at least two meals a day. He babbled cheerfully to her about the day's events and, when Bree could not tolerate idle chatter, he sat beside her in silence. Understanding her connection to the land, he dragged her out of bed and walked her to her favorite park, so she could sit beneath the oak trees. He had even driven Bree to the airport when the pain of life in Saint Louis without Gwen became too much.

Fergus hesitated. "I was hoping you might come home soon."

"Home," Bree chuckled. "You mean, back to Saint Louis."

"Well, yeah."

He loved her.

Gwen was right, Bree admitted, picking at the wool socks beside her.

In the years since her friendship with Fergus started, Gwen had teased Bree about their relationship. "Say hello to your boyfriend for me," she would call as Bree walked out the door to meet him at the café. But Bree had never taken her seriously. No, Gwen was the only one Bree had wanted or thought of as a lover.

She still did, despite Gwen's ghostly visit at Seattle airport three months ago.

"He loves you," Gwen had whispered from the seat next to Bree, her soul form gesturing to Bree's ringing telephone. *"Answer it. Answer it, with my blessing."*

Bree could still see Gwen sitting there, Otherworldly bright and smiling amongst the other airline passengers.

"Trust in Love again," Gwen had urged.

Bree sighed. As usual, Gwen had seen through to the Truth. She had known all along—Fergus loved her.

He had never said as much, but Bree now knew it was true. The thought sent heat pulsing through her. Her energy body tingled as her heart raced, and she scowled.

Beyond a few curious kisses, Bree had never been drawn to men. She could appreciate their fierce beauty, even enjoy a harmless moment of flirtation, but a man had never held her interest beyond the trifling. And she had never thought of Fergus as a man. Until now.

"Bree?"

Soft and sensual with the feathery touch of a lover's lips, Fergus's voice drifted down Bree's neck. She shivered as her heart raced. *Strange,* she frowned. *Could I possibly love him*?

"I have to do this, Fergus."

Fergus sighed through the telephone. In Bree's inner vision, hazel eyes closed slowly as fiery, red hair spilled to fill her view.

"For her, or for you?"

He sees through me to the Truth. Bree closed her eyes. *Just like Gwen did.*

"For us both."

"Okay. Just answer me this—are you ever coming home?"

It was Bree's turn to sigh. She shook her head, as if he were sitting there with her and could see her. "Honestly, Fergus, I don't know where home is anymore."

6

Bree stood in the shadow of the hawthorn tree, at the far edge of Brighid's sacred enclosure in the Kildare countryside. Letting her gaze drift along the limbs closest to the ground, Bree considered the endless bits of ribbon and cloth covering the branches. Each colorful string, she knew, was tied intentionally to the tree and carried the prayer of a person or a community.

Clooties, the Irish called them. A prayer entrusted to the magic of the elements—earth, air, fire, water and ether—for manifestation.

A tradition as old as the Irish people, Bree thought. *And a magic even older.*

Bree lifted her gaze to track the limbs and branches just above her head. Here, too, small pieces of colorful cloth danced in the breeze.

With a sigh, Bree reached into her left pocket and drew out a thin strip of white, cotton cloth, about six inches in length. The long edges were frayed and the escaping threads shimmied with the wind. She had torn the piece from the Brighid's mantle she set outside for the goddess to bless in February.

"This is my promise to you," Brighid's voice whispered from the past to flow anew within Bree. *"Each Imbolc I shall return to wake*

the sleeping life force, to summon it up and out of the womb of the earth, and to restore warmth to cover the earth in green." Golden light had blazed in Bree's inner vision as the goddess walked barefoot upon the frozen earth, leaving green stems rising out of the soil behind Her and filling Her footprints with small, white buds. *"Look for me when the snowdrop blossoms and the ewes flow with milk."*

"The night before the rising of my fire," Bríghid's voice flowed on, *"place a white cloth upon the earth. During my walk to awaken the earth, I will touch the cloth and fill it with my healing light, imbue it with my blessing of Love. This shall be my gift to you."*

Bríghid had been true to Her word. Each February on Bríghid's Day Eve, Bree placed two pieces of white cloth outside for Bríghid's blessing—one for use on her personal altar, and one that she tore into thin strips for her clients. *A special Irish blessing,* she would tell them as she wrapped the cotton *clootie* around their wrists.

Not this time, she thought, twining the strip around her right index finger. Today, she had a different purpose in mind.

Stretching to reach an open spot, Bree tied the *clootie* to a limb of the hawthorn tree. *For Peace between me and Mother Bríghid,* she prayed silently as she watched the white threads dance in the breeze. Then, with a sigh, she stepped away from the tree.

"I am sorry, Mother. I did not mean to argue with you."

Warmth, firm and tender, brushed lovingly against her left side, nuzzling in slow circles at her waist. Her eyes fixed on the white *clootie,* Bree lowered her left hand and stroked the fur of her Bear Ally.

"She knows," Bear whispered.

A gust of wind set the limbs of the hawthorn to swaying, and Bree watched the bits of cloth and string flutter. The riot of colors shimmied side to side, blurring into a rainbow. Bree stroked her Ally and wondered.

Does She really?

Bree dropped her gaze to the left. Bear stood there on all fours, black eyes looking up at her. As Bree turned toward her Ally, Bear rose onto her hind legs and rested her paws upon Bree's chest. Leaning into the contact, Bree touched her nose to the soft leather of Bear's snout. She remained there, just breathing nose to nose with Bear, sharing their traditional welcome.

"She does, of course." Bear's voice echoed through Bree's awareness. *"You are Her Love, Bree Nic Bhríde."*

Bree frowned and drew her head back, gently breaking the contact with Bear before stepping away fully.

As Bear settled back onto all fours, Bree turned and walked through the enclosure, past her favorite willow seat toward the line of five, knee-high stones that stretched across the earth to the flowing waters of Bríghid's spring. Beside her, she could hear the grass purring with each step of her Ally.

Stopping before the fifth stone, Bree let the fingertips of her left hand drift over the rough surface.

"We call these stones the Chakras of Bríghid..." A woman's voice pulled Bree into memory. *"One for Being. Two for Creating. Three for Loving. Four for Tending. Five for Seeing. Each stone embodies a unique aspect of the goddess, but only in contemplating all five may you awaken Her Love within you."*

Bree had never met the woman before, nor had she seen the woman since. The woman simply walked up to Bree one day and started talking. When Bree asked what had inspired the woman to speak to her, the woman smiled and replied, *"Bríghid asked me to."* Bree could still see the soft fullness of the woman's face and the kindness shining in the eyes.

"Remember," the woman had paused to say before leaving, *"The heart beats at the center. And every journey to Bríghid is a journey to the heart."*

Lifting her gaze, Bree counted. *Five... four... three.* Fixing her eyes on her destination, Bree let her fingertips slide along the rough surfaces as she walked past each stone to the one at the center.

The heart of Bríghid, she whispered mentally, then sat on the ground in front of the stone.

The grass humming softly, Bear settled next to her. Without thinking, Bree wrapped her left arm around her Ally.

Bree closed her eyes and exhaled slowly. Sinking into the

stillness, she listened for the heartbeat of the Goddess, the Great Mother of Life. In its place, three words sang a constant refrain.

"Bree Nic Bhríde... Bree Nic Bhríde... Bree Nic Bhríde."

"Why does She call me that?" Bree wondered aloud.

Her Bear Ally shifted beside her. Bree opened her eyes to find black eyes staring at her. *"Bree Nic Bhríde?"*

Bree nodded.

A breeze drifted through Bree's hair as her Ally sighed, head lowering to rest upon Bree's left knee. *"Because it is your name."*

Bree frowned. A frisson of anger rushed from her core out to the edges of her being, and she shivered.

Bear lifted her head and turned again toward Bree. *"You misunderstand, chiya. It is your Gaelic name."*

Wrinkling her brow, Bree gazed harshly into her Ally's black eyes. "What do you mean?"

"You should study your Gaelic more thoroughly." Bear lifted her snout and nuzzled Bree's chin tenderly. *"Bree Nic Bhríde... in Gaelic it means Bree, daughter of Bríde. In the past, here on this isle, this is how the people would have called you. Whether you choose to recognize it or not, Daughter of Bríde, this is who you are."*

Bree stared at the heart stone. *Daughter of Bríde...* She let the words wash over her.

Two vibrations pulsed within that name, both calling to her. Sinking into the rhythm, she saw her mother, a smile blazing across her face as she laughed heartily. The laughter stretched and blended into the sound of her mother humming a lullaby as she rocked Bree as a small babe in her arms. Bríde was the name of her biological mother in this lifetime. That made her, literally, Bree Nic Bhríde.

In her inner vision, her mother looked up and smiled as golden light blazed, filling Bree's awareness. That light danced and rippled until the face of Bríghid emerged. Bree gasped. Bríde, she remembered, was a variation of the name Bríghid. In some Gaelic communities, the goddess Bríghid was known as Bríde. As a *Bean feasa*, Bree was a Daughter of Bríghid, a Daughter of Bríde.

"Bree Nic Bhríde." Bree spoke the name aloud and let it wash over her.

Deep inside her, part of her soul shook and retorted angrily, *Bree MacLeod.*

Bree sighed. "Yes, that is true. But it seems I am this, too."

Inside her, that angry Bree huffed but relented, stepping to the side as she folded her arms over her chest. Not yielding entirely, she stood there, glaring.

Stroking the fur of her Bear Ally, Bree tried again. "Bree Nic Bhríde."

This time the vibration ached and swelled, calling to Bree and filling her with a powerful yearning. To her surprise, she wanted to dive into that pulsation, to drink deeply of its flowing and let it shape her.

Staring at the center stone, she wondered aloud, "But what will become of Bree MacLeod?"

7

Bree wove her way through the parking lot of Inverness Airport. The keys to her rental car jangling in her hand, she spotted the electric-blue Citroën C1 from at least twelve feet away. The sign above it made her smile. Hertz, Car 9.

Pulling her suitcase up to rest behind her, she stood before the sign and chuckled. "The trine of the Trine, and brilliant blue. Thank you, Mother Bríghid, for Your sacred shelter."

Still grinning, Bree collapsed the handle down on her suitcase before tucking it into the Citroën's tiny, rear compartment. Luggage stowed, she walked around the car, checking for any damage. Satisfied with the condition of the car, she opened the left front door and leaned in, settling her purse onto the passenger seat. Reaching into the inside pocket, she pulled out a silver flask about the size of her palm. Three dragons spiraled across the flask's surface, their tails disappearing into endless, interlocking curls.

Bree unscrewed the top and breathed in the peaty fragrance. "*Uisce beatha...* The Waters of Life," she breathed. With a brief smile, she raised the flask up before her and closed her eyes.

"Mother Alba, Blessed Scotia and Guardians of this land, I send you gentle greetings. A child of your people, I come to Your domains in Peace, in Love and by invitation of one of Your own." She emptied a pour of whiskey onto the parking lot beside the Citroën. "And I make this offering only to honor, always to honor and to honor all ways." Righting the flask, she continued. "I ask for the blessing of Your sacred hospitality, Your loving refuge and peaceful shelter for the duration of my stay in Your lands. I ask this in Peace, in Love and in gentle gratitude."

Bree drew the open flask back to her chest and waited.

"Crrruck!" A raven called from overhead. Bree opened her eyes and lifted her gaze. Vast, black wings trembled as they spiraled through the sky above her.

"Be ye welcomed, Daughter of Bríde, blood of the Sídhe, and child of MacLeod." The words poured through Bree, spilling upon her soul and setting her body to shiver. *"Be ye welcomed in Love."*

Bree closed her eyes and bowed her head. The motherly voice flowed like a river, pulling Bree beyond This World into light, clear and sparkling. Eyes, bright as the summer sky, shone before her. Drifting in their depths, two white lines crossed within the shimmering blue as the Saltire, the flag of Scotland, blazed.

"Mother Scotia?" Bree's voice was a whisper.

"Be ye welcomed." The voice pooled around Bree as hands—callused yet gentle—wove a single raven feather into Bree's hair. *"Go with my blessing and walk upon my lands in Peace."*

The Otherworldly feather danced in the breeze, brushing the top of Bree's shoulder. "*Sin é,*" she whispered.

"*Sin è,*" the voice flowed, clear and sparkling.

"Crrruck!"

Opening her eyes to This World, Bree lifted her gaze skyward. Black feathers stretched and spiraled far above her. "Thank you, too, Raven," she nodded, addressing her Ally. The wings tipped and swayed side-to-side above her.

Bree replaced the cap onto the flask and opened the right-side door to the Citroën. She settled herself in the driver's seat, then leaned toward her purse. After returning the flask to the inside pocket, she rummaged a bit deeper and pulled out a thin, six-inch strip of white, cotton cloth. Tying the *clootie* around the stem of the rearview mirror, Bree called to her Teacher. "Mother Bríghid, blessed Keeper of the Sacred Flame, please bless, shelter and carry me, this vehicle and my belongings in Your Love, Your Light, Your sacred Grace."

"Crrruck!"

The raven swept down and landed upon the hood of the Citroën. Tucking its massive wings, the bird stood staring at Bree. Its eyes, she noticed, were level with her own. As her gaze tracked the long curve of its beak, she reached a finger to trace her much smaller nose. Dropping her hand back to her lap, she shook her head and blinked. "You make an unusual hood ornament."

"Bonnet, not hood."

The unfamiliar, mental voice pierced through Bree's awareness so fast, she wondered if she had actually heard it. She leaned closer to the windshield and peered into unflinching, black eyes. "Well, if you're comfortable, I am grateful."

The raven shifted from talon to talon, then shivered as it perched itself on the hood of her rental car, its black eyes staring at Bree.

"Thank you." Bree nodded specifically to the raven, then lifted her eyes. "And thank You, Mother Scotia and Mother Bríghid."

Bree picked the car key out of her purse, disengaged the clutch and started the Citroën. Popping the shift into neutral, she let the car run while she pulled the seatbelt across her and clicked it into the lock to her left. Facing forward again, she gazed into the watchful, black eyes of the raven as the Otherworldly feather brushed her shoulder.

Gripping the wheel with both hands, she sighed. "Okay, Allies. I am here. Show me the way."

8

"Crrruck!" The raven spread its wings and jumped into flight as Bree put the Citroën in gear and pulled out of the Inverness Airport parking lot.

She followed the C1017 through three traffic circles, then merged onto the A96 heading south toward the city of Inverness. She knew the Moray Firth stretched out of sight off to her right. With a smile, she exhaled, letting her awareness flow outward in search of the local waters.

The sound of metal ringing against metal clattered through her and Bree jumped. Blood-soaked hair splattered across her face and into her mouth. She tried to spit it out, but there was nothing there. She looked in the rear-view mirror and found only her reflection staring wildly back at her.

She shifted her gaze back to the road as the ringing of metal burst through her awareness once again. The colors hung heavy on her, sweat-soaked and bloody, and her arms burned with fatigue. But she would not stop. A sword cut toward her and her arms shook, muscles bunching painfully as she blocked the blade.

Bree gripped the hilt hard and gasped at the curve of the wheel in her hands. *What is happening?*

With a quick glance behind her, she guided the car to the side of the road. Her breath came hard and fast, as the sound of grunting filled her ears. She was sure her feet were mired in blood and mud, but she could clearly see her clean, square-toed boots on the clutch and brake pedals. Fighting to steady her breathing, she shifted into neutral, pressed both feet onto the brake and dropped her head against the steering wheel. Tears spilled hot and fierce down her cheeks as her vision blurred.

Muscles burn with relentless effort and the grunting deepens. Somewhere blood oozes, spilling down a shaking thigh. Muscles bunch as the sword swings once more. Another block. Another parry, despite the growing sense of certain defeat.

"Too few," a gruff voice rumbles into the slash. Metal rings out, clashing with metal, silenced as it bites to cut. "Too few."

With a grunt, he sinks claymore through flesh once more. But he knows. The battle is lost.

Metal pierces his chest and he gasps as battle-weary flesh tenses once more. His struggle sends the tear deeper until muscles rend and yield. In the falling silence, Bree hears only the wind crying through the heather as the image of a woman—tall, broad-shouldered with long, black hair whipping in the wind—turns hazel eyes upon her.

"No," Bree realizes, "upon him. It's the man she sees."

Knees buckle, returning the body to earth. "Tha bròn orm... I'm sorry..." escapes as a grunt. As his last breath casts itself to the wind, the woman closes her eyes and walks away.

Bree gasped through sobs, forehead pressing upon the steering wheel of the rented Citroën. Pain seared through her body as the blue of her jeans blurred into view. She blinked her eyes, trying to clear them.

"What is this?"

"Crrruck!"

Bree lifted her tear-soaked face to see Raven perched on top of the road sign a few feet in front of her car. The word "Culloden" stretched below her Ally.

Her mouth dropped open and she panted. "Culloden Moor... is here?"

Raven nodded and jutted her beak eastward toward a tree-covered hill.

Bree gripped the steering wheel, her body shaking visibly. "Am... Am I to go there?" Her words were a breathless whisper.

Raven turned Otherworldly black eyes upon Bree. *"Not today, Raven Child."*

Bree wept. Her tears wrenched themselves loudly from her chest, her body shuddering with each convulsion. As the flood finally slowed, Bree sat back and wiped her eyes. Her Raven Ally sat on the hood of the Citroën watching her.

"Sometimes remembering is enough." Raven launched herself into the air and headed south. *"Come, Raven Child. She is waiting for you."*

9

Bree exhaled and ran a trembling hand through her hair. As the exit to the A9 came into view, a wave of gratitude flooded through her. Heading west out of the traffic circle, she glanced into her rearview mirror and watched the road to Culloden disappear. The skin of her cheeks pulled taut from the salt of her tears and she considered splashing some water on her face to ease the discomfort.

What about their pain, she rued. *All those clansmen... slaughtered.* Two thousand men shed their lifeblood for Bonnie Prince Charlie on Culloden moor. It was April 16th, 1746. They fought the English crown for the honor of the Highland way and died in less than an hour. Her face contorted as fresh tears spilled softly down her cheeks. *Their way of life died with them on that field.*

"*Tha bròn orm... I'm sorry...*" The voice from her vision echoed.

Hazel eyes blazed through Bree's awareness as black hair whipped in the wind. *The woman from my vision,* Bree breathed. Expressionless, the woman gazed across an open field covered in heather. Her lover would never cross that field again, nor would he kiss her hotly upon that earth. Lifting her chin, the woman turned her back to the field and disappeared.

Could she know everything she held dear would disappear too?

With the blood of the clans still pooling on Culloden moor, the Highland way of life was declared outlaw and everything withered.

"*Tha bròn orm... I'm sorry...*" The clansman's voice echoed.

Bree shook herself, forcibly breaking the connection to the vision. "They wanted a sovereign of their own kith and kin," she breathed. "They never had a chance." Fresh tears scattered across the backs of her hands.

The sign for the A82 blurred into view and Bree steered through the traffic circle and onto the highway. Skirting the city of Inverness, Bree headed south out of town and toward the shores of Loch Ness itself. She half hoped the local Water Horse might make an appearance along the drive. After the metallic sting of Culloden, Nessie would be a refreshing encounter.

The steel and grey of the city receded and the trees of the Great Glen stretched open arms to welcome her. Following the roadway into the dense shelter, Bree sighed gustily, her shoulders slumping with relief. The thrumming presence of the wood spirits smoothed a loving balm upon her aching soul and she let the road carry her a while.

10

Bree steered the blue Citroën across *an Drochaid an Eilein Sgitheanaich*, or what the English-speaking locals called the Skye Bridge. Her trip along the waters of Loch Ness had proved peaceful, not a Water Kelpie in sight.

She had encountered what she could only call *a presence*. Deep and ancient, it had sent Goddess-bumps shivering across her skin and, somewhere near the village of Drumnadrochit, she knew for certain—the waters were watching her. Now, as she followed the A87 across the bridge to the Isle of Skye, the waters of Loch Alsh nipped and snapped below her. Biting in her direction, Bree wondered if she had angered them somehow.

"It does nay seem respectful," Caitlìn had told Bree before her departure, "taking a bridge across the waters that keep our Isle. For centuries the waters themselves chose to carry or no those who attempted to ford or ferry them. Ye had to make a proper asking of them. Now, ye just roll across them, with nary a word or offering." Her kinswoman had sighed harshly. "Does nay seem natural, certainly no' for a MacLeod."

"Where is the closest ferry, then?" Bree had asked. She had no intention of insulting her ancestors, much less the local water spirits.

"Time was Kyle of Lochalsh would have been the place." Caitlìn's voice fell silent.

"And now?"

"Ach... well... there's a ferry there now, sure. But it won't carry ye anywhere." Caitlìn grunted in disgust.

"Why not?"

"Too few would pay precious coin to ferry the waters when the bridge would carry for free. So it stands closed—one more relic, another vestige of life lost to history." Caitlìn had sighed. "Today, ye can only cross by the bridge."

Sunlight glinted, breaking through the grey of the clouds and reflecting off the silver surface of Bree's flask. It had slipped out of the inner pocket of her purse and sat now in the open center of the bag. In the flashing light, the dragons seemed to stretch their tails and spiral across its surface.

"Sometimes remembering is enough," the dragons whispered, their eyes following Bree.

"Go raibh mille maith agaibh... Thank you," she winked.

The blue Citroën cleared the bridge, making landfall onto the Isle of Skye, the ancestral homeland of clan MacLeod. As the guardrail fell away, Bree spied a graveled area overlooking the waters, and she pulled the rental car off the two-lane road. Grabbing the flask from her purse, she opened the car door and set her feet on the earth of her ancestors.

Inside her boots, her toes tingled as voices whispered and echoed through her awareness. *Peace to you,* she called to the voices as she walked around the car and stood on the slope where the gravel gave way to earthy peat. Then, bending her knees, she settled into a crouch. She touched fingertips to lips and pressed the kiss upon the rocky soil. *Blessed is the Mother.*

Bree gazed out across the waters of Loch Alsh. White caps still nipped and snapped in her direction and she bowed to them. "Blessed waters," she began, unscrewing the top of her flask. "Once I would have sought your blessing before entrusting myself to your welcome and your safe-passage by boat. But time dances and ways change. Today, the bridge offers the only crossing. Please forgive." She emptied a pour of whiskey upon the soil. "And know this: I remember, and I honor you."

Drawing the flask close against her chest, Bree closed her eyes. "I honor you."

Black hair drifted around her shoulders as a breeze rose off the waters. *"Blessings, Raven Child, Blood of the Sìdhe. Be ye welcomed and walk ye here in Peace. For in Peace are ye sheltered on our isle."*

"Tapadh libh... Thank you," Bree whispered, eyes still closed.

Replacing the top on her flask, Bree stood up from her crouch and gazed out across the waters. The white caps now gone, the sun glistened and rippled across the gently flowing loch. She bowed again, her right hand over her heart. "Blessed is the Mystery."

Bree walked back toward her rental car. The sun spilled down upon the Citroën, haloing it in a blazing, neon-blue aura. Bree stopped and stood, her mouth gaping in awe.

"You were happy here."

Bree pivoted, spinning in place and expecting to find someone behind her. Sunlight glinted upon the quiet waters of the loch, but she was alone on the roadside. Images churned through her inner awareness. Two men in kilts—one tall, thin and fair-haired, the other dark-haired and broad-shouldered—leaned against each other as they laughed. *Blood-brothers.* The word rang through Bree even as the image spotted and blurred. Colors swirled through her inner vision, pooling to reveal familiar, hazel eyes and a square jaw surrounded with black hair.

It's her, Bree breathed. *The woman from my vision.*

A smile, tender and inviting, spread across the woman's face as the black-haired man with broad shoulders grazed her hand with a kiss. *"Mo ghràidh... My love..."* his voice, deep and rumbling, tumbled through Bree.

Her heart pounded. *The clansman with the sword. But who? Who is he?*

The breeze tossed her hair. *"He is you. Or, you were him."*

Bree's chin itched. She reached to scratch the coarse, dark beard she knew should grow there, but her chin was bare. She looked up to see the hazel-eyed woman smiling softly, her face drawing closer until lips, soft and inviting, grazed in loving caress.

Heat flooded through her, reaching from lips to heart, hands and feet.

Sunlight flashed off the water's surface, and the ghostly image of two men on horseback shimmered into view. One muscular with copper-colored hair and painted lines spiraling down his face to his left arm, the other dark-haired with sharp, steel-grey eyes and broad shoulders. The men drew their horses to a rest and dismounted. Their kilts billowing in the sea breeze, they pulled canteens, bannock, and dried meat from their packs. In easy silence they settled themselves amongst the rocks and passed food and water between them. Bree's left hand reached toward the top of her boot as the copper-haired man drew a *sgian dubh*, a short knife, from the hose above his left legging.

"You were happy here."

Startled, Bree swung back toward the road. The rocky hills stretched west toward the horizon as the rental car sat quietly waiting. She was alone.

Heart pounding in her chest, Bree looked back over her shoulder, but the two men and their horses had disappeared.

11

"Oh, Caitlìn, it's lovely!"

Bree stood in the den of Heather House, her kinswoman's bed and breakfast near the village of Dunvegan. Through the large bay window, the western wall of the traditional one-and-a-half-height stone building shone brilliant white in the sunlight glinting off Loch Dunvegan. Gazing across the waters, Bree could see the ancient hill, known to the locals and MacLeods the world over as MacLeod's Tables.

The room, like the others she had seen on the ground floor, was clean, cozy and welcoming, complete with overstuffed sofas and a fireplace. The low ceiling and earth tones of the décor enfolded her in a warm embrace, and she suddenly longed to put her feet up and linger a while.

"Ye should ha' seen it before," Caitlìn groaned.

Still admiring the simple comfort of the room—lavender- and sage-colored throw pillows offering a gentle accent over the earth-toned curtains and floor rug—Bree noticed her friend walk over to the cabinet in the corner and open the top drawer. Closing the drawer, Caitlìn turned and handed her a book of photos.

"A right mess it was when Mother bought it. Took me a year to complete the renovations, then another year to figure out how to market it."

Bree leafed through the pages. The photos tracked the conversion of a run-down, junk-filled, traditional stone house into a bright and welcoming bed and breakfast. She looked up and shook her head.

"If it was such a mess, why did she buy it?"

Caitlìn smiled and ran her gaze along the wood-trimmed ceiling. "Her best friend from childhood grew up here. She said the place had some fine memories, and she could use a few more of those."

Bree furrowed her eyebrows and shook her head at her friend.

"I came with her, after she bought it—sight unseen, mind—and moved here. I did nay plan to stay... Ach, well, ye know how that goes." Caitlìn nodded and sighed. "She stood out front, weeds up to her knees, gazing at the doorway as if it were a gateway to the World of the Fae itself. I can still see her—hands on her hips and that lopsided grin spilling across her face. She was so proud of the place, ramshackle though it was."

Bree watched the smile on her kinswoman's face fall downward into a frown, her chin drooping toward the floor.

"Then she said, '*Bha thusa ceàrr, a mhàthair*...You were wrong, Mother. I said I'd be back, and I am.'"

"What did she mean?"

Caitlìn's gaze snapped back into focus and she shrugged. "Gran dinnae approve of Mother marrying outside of Skye. Mother would always ask how things were back home. Gran would always answer the same. 'Ach, what would ye care? Ye've left and there's an end to it.'" Caitlìn shook her head. "It used to drive Mother to tears."

Bree closed the book of photos and placed it on the wooden coffee table. "What brought her back to Skye?"

"Longing."

Caitlìn picked up the book of photos and returned it to the cabinet drawer. "After Father died, all she wanted was to go home. Said she'd lived in exile long enough." Caitlìn sighed. Sliding her hands into the back pockets of her jeans, she walked up to the window overlooking the loch. "I always knew she missed life here, though I did nay realize how much. I'd never seen her so happy— pulling weeds, cutting peat and chasing birds from the thatching."

Bree watched her kinswoman gaze silently through the window into the past. *How many others*, she wondered, *have stood just there, eyes cast beyond glass and water, across mountain and heather, searching? How many of those had returned, aching for that view, that earth, their souls singing them home?*

Longing, Bree dropped her gaze to the floor. *What better reason to stop wandering?*

Her eyes traced the weave of the rug, flowing along the earth-colored ridges to the strings gathered and tied into endless tassels. Drifting along the edge, her vision blurred as voices flooded through her.

Laughter, loud and raucous, resounded with the deep tones of men and the soft rushes of women. She could almost see them—shadows stretched to fill the room, outlines of the past, rising with the crackle of the hearth fire and the husky smell of burning peat. The laughter drifted to silence as the sound of a woman humming spilled through her awareness. The soft sway of a rocker creaked and soothing radiance seeped from the fire to color the house in golden warmth.

Bathed in that comfort, Bree exhaled deeply. But the color slowly drained, fading to leave the room forgotten, lost in greys and shadows, the rocking chair broken and buried in dust.

The voice of Caitlìn's mother whispered through Bree.

"'A wee bit of tenderness and lovin'—'tis all it needs...'" Bree nodded to her friend. "That's what your mother would have said."

Caitlìn chuckled and shook her head. "She would and she did."

Bree smiled as her kinswoman faced her. "And she was right."

"She often was." Caitlìn sighed. "C'mon, I'll show ye the rest of the place."

12

"Should ye have need of anything while I'm in Cape Breton, ye can rely on Màire MacLeod." Caitlìn steered her Land Rover along the A863 toward the heart of Dunvegan village. "She keeps her own place, the Sea Rose, in Stein. 'Tis a lovely old inn on Loch Bay, just up the road from Heather House, in Waternish."

Caitlìn slowed down as they passed the police station and tourist information center set just off the road in the narrow village. Bree saw a woman with long red hair wave from outside the general store. "Maggie MacKenzie, hullo," Caitlìn called through the open window as she returned the greeting.

"A fine day to ye!" Warmth hugged Bree's shoulders as Maggie's voice drifted through the front of the Rover.

As the truck rolled through the snug town center, nods and friendly gestures greeted them from every doorstep. A smile lit the face of a young man, his curly brown hair spilling out from under a green, knitted cap. Caitlìn smiled in return and, watching the exchange, Bree's vision blurred. Light—golden and luminous— flowed in vibrant threads, rippling from his heart to touch Caitlìn's. Bree heard her kinswoman laugh and saw the light shimmer back along the threads to enfold the young man in brilliance. Bree shifted her gaze. All around her, threads of radiance rippled, reaching from heart to heart and bathing the locals in golden light.

Her vision shifted back to This World and she smiled. The one- and two-story buildings around her offered no signs of "civilization." No Tesco markets, no House of Fraser department stores nor any of the usual restaurants and shops. Even the police station and post office were housed in simple stone buildings that seemed to rise out of the local earth more than the twenty-first century. But, with the light of those threads gleaming fresh in her memory, she understood. This place offered something more. It offered *belonging*.

A sign announcing the approach of the A850 blurred past her. Attempting to read it, she almost missed the red flash of the stop sign ahead. The Land Rover heaved to the right as the road curved suddenly and dead-ended into a t-stop. Caitlin braked hard and Bree braced herself against the dashboard. Her eyes bulged at the enormous stone retaining wall looming directly where the road should continue. Mouth slowly gaping, Bree tracked the endless rows of stones up to the broad hill towering above her. As the truck shuddered to a stop, her gaze reached the summit and she gasped.

Kilt billowing green, blue and yellow in the breeze, the old man stood on top of the hill. Reaching out from the Otherworld, his gaze locked with hers. Bree tried to look away, but his grey eyes refused to release hers. As the thrum of a heartbeat ached through her awareness, she tried to blink but could only stare. The fingers of her left hand curled into a fist as the old man grasped the staff in his left hand and beckoned her with the other.

"Come. She is waiting for you."

The Land Rover lurched as Caitlin shifted into a hard right turn onto the A850. Unable to look away, Bree watched the man gesturing to her. She craned her neck to the left as the hill passed out of sight. Still the connection between her and the man continued to pull on her awareness, and she found herself panting softly. As the truck rounded the next bend in the road, the link suddenly snapped and she rocked in her seat.

Steadying herself against the dashboard, Bree shifted to face forward and glanced toward her kinswoman. Caitlìn calmly steered the Land Rover along the curving, two-way road that passed as a highway on Skye. Her eyes were focused and intent while her energy field shimmered hooded. Bree settled back in her seat and wondered what her friend might know about the old man on the hill. As she debated asking, a truck drifted over the middle line and Caitlìn swerved to avoid hitting it. Lurching with the Rover, Bree reconsidered.

Best let her drive in peace, she decided.

Beyond her window, the peaty braes of northwestern Skye rose and fell, windswept and rocky. They whispered of stories forgotten and untold, but Bree could see only the grey eyes of the old man. They shone clear and bright as the moon in her awareness and she knew they were watching her, even now.

Who is he? She called to her Otherworldly Allies.

"He is one of the Ancient Ones, one of the People of Peace," Raven's voice whispered in her awareness, *"and he is the Guardian of this place."*

One of the Sìdhe? Bree wondered. *What does he want with me?*

"Remember who you are, chiya," the voice of her Bear Ally rippled through her. *"Remember and discover the Truth hidden within you."*

The Land Rover slowed and Caitlìn steered a quick left, heading north on the B886. Shifting her gaze back to the road ahead, Bree caught the glance her kinswoman cast in her direction.

"She is expecting us." Caitlìn nodded. "Màire, that is. I thought it best the two of ye meet."

Bree glanced at the dashboard clock and chuckled. *Just up the road...* They had been traveling at least fifteen minutes already.

She smiled at her kinswoman. "Is Màire family?"

"Not exactly."

Caitlìn downshifted and turned left onto a small, island roadway. In the distance, a dozen white stone buildings clustered along the edge of a short, single-lane road opposite a green slope that cascaded down to the sea. An old crofters' village, the buildings were beautifully restored and gleamed in the noon-day sun.

Caitlìn pointed toward a traditional white inn with windows tucked under three eaves. "That's it there."

"How did you meet?"

"She came to Heather House after I returned from Mother's funeral. She'd read the notice in the local paper and came to offer her respects. Seems they were friends, in *ye olde daes*." Caitlìn shrugged. "She's been kind to me. And ye can trust her, should ye need help with the inn."

Bree felt the Land Rover slow as the road curved and narrowed. She doubted two cars could pass abreast here and wondered what the pace of life might be like in this time-forgotten hamlet. As they entered the village, a couple out for a walk waved casually and Bree returned the gesture with a nod. The riot of colors thriving in the gardens on the sea-side of the road dazzled her and she almost missed the speed limit sign.

"Welcome to Stein," it read, "where twenty's plenty."

13

"Just wha' we need, another *Sasannach* on our Isle."

"Màire MacLeod," Caitlìn scowled, her fists reaching for her hips. "Since when is a MacLeod a stranger, much less a *Sasannach* and unwelcome to Skye?"

Màire arched one eyebrow and lifted her chin. "Since she speaks with an American accent."

They stood in the gleaming kitchen of the Sea Rose. Despite the fire burning in the hearth, Bree shivered and drew her fleece jacket more tightly around her. *Sasannach...* the word bristled in her awareness and chilled the edges of her energy field. While the Gaelic word formally meant Englishman, it was used more commonly to mean outsider, interloper and one who did not belong.

Fire blazed deep within Bree and the angry part of her soul retorted. *Who is she to disrespect a MacLeod?*

"My father's people came from Skye." The words were out of her mouth before Bree could stop them. Her breath came a little too fast, and she forced herself to unclench the fists balled in her pockets.

In haunting slow motion, Bree watched the angular chin and narrowed eyes turn and lock on her.

"*Did* they, now?"

Màire took a step toward Bree, then another. The sound of swords rattling wooden shields echoed through her awareness. For a moment, she could feel her body tensed and ready for combat, the hilt of a sword gripped in her hand. She blinked, and both sword and shield were gone.

"And can ye show me the lands they called their own? The soil they tilled and worked with their bare hands?"

Images danced through Bree's inner vision. Green earth, tumbling over rolling hills and a small cottage nestled beside a pond pooling from a natural spring. Just beyond the cottage, a stone path meandered down the hill to pause along the free-flowing waters of a loch. Deep basso tones hummed as a man's broad hands broke open the earth for planting. She would know the place if and when she saw it. But, could she declare its location?

At her sides, her fists balled anew. "Not exactly."

Màire scowled, pressing her thin lips tight.

Is she right? Bree wondered. *Does place of birth determine belonging? Can a patch of turf long ago lost reclaim what was forsaken? Can a connection to something that was deem a place home now?*

Hazel eyes blurred into view in her inner vision. She watched a half-smile crease the left side of a man's weathered face, his copper-colored hair flowing as painted lines spiraled down his cheek, shoulder and arm. Hands on his hips, the muscular man shook his head. *"MacLeod Ye were borne, and MacLeod Ye are todae. 'Tis good enough for Chief and clan. Ye remember tha' now and always."*

Bree blinked and opened her eyes to Màire's slits. "The MacLeod would bid me welcome."

"The more the fool he." Màire scoffed and shook her head. "The Chief would welcome every last one of ye, offspring of those who left, ye who had no stay..."

"*Exiles...*" The unspoken word chilled Bree to her core and she shivered.

"Màire," Caitlìn placed a hand on the woman's shoulder. "I'm asking ye for help."

The woman scowled and turned to face her kinswoman. "And because ye ask it, Caitlìn MacLeod of Skye, *Sasannach* or no, she shall have it."

14

Caitlìn downshifted and steered the Land Rover through the right-hand turn onto the A850, heading back to Dunvegan. Bree caught the sideways glance from her kinswoman and sighed. Neither of them had spoken since Caitlìn had bid farewell to Màire and the Sea Rose. Bree was glad for the quiet.

"I'm sorry, Bree." Caitlìn turned a quick gaze in her direction, then back to the two-lane road. "I did nay know... did nay expect..."

Màire's narrowed eyes scowled through Bree's inner vision. *"Sasannach."* Cold and accusing, the word spilled ice down her spine.

"She was so.... *hostile.*" Bree shook her head slowly, her eyes on the road ahead. She certainly was no stranger to being unwelcome. Her uncle had taught her that lesson at an early age. And her recent visit to Seattle had only reinforced his hatred. But to be called *that word* by a kinswoman... Bree shivered and closed her eyes.

"Tha bròn orm... I'm sorry..." The clansman's voice echoed from the Otherworld.

"I'm sorry." Caitlìn's voice flowed soft and gentle, and Bree turned to face her kinswoman. "She hae always been so helpful, taught me much about welcoming guests. I thought she would look after ye for me, even be a friend to ye."

Bree nodded. "Well, you'll forgive me, I hope, if I do not call her. For anything."

Caitlìn barked a laugh. "I would nay question why ye chose not to."

Bree looked out her window and let her gaze drift. Low, rocky hills rolled in all directions and her vision blurred softly with the speed of the Land Rover. As the truck rounded a curve in the road, a presence tugged at her awareness. Shifting her gaze, Bree blinked slowly, her mouth gaping.

There, at the top of the same hill, she could clearly see the old man. The yellow stripes of his kilt shone in the sunlight, radiant against the blue and green of his plaid and the earth. Leaning against the staff in his left hand, he beckoned to her.

"Come. She is waiting for you."

Bree sat up in her seat, staring.

Following her gaze, Caitlìn nodded as the truck slowed. "That's the Duirnish Stone."

Bree faced her kinswoman and frowned. "Stone? But... I see a man."

Caitlìn grunted and shook her head as she downshifted, preparing to turn left onto the A863. "I should ha' known ye would see him." She changed her blinker from left to right and pulled a hard u-turn, heading back along the A850.

Bree gripped the dashboard handle to steady herself as a gravel pullout came into view on the left. This time Bree was prepared when her kinswoman steered the Land Rover into it and stopped in front of the hill.

"It's a steep climb, the tor is," Caitlìn pointed to the hill and nodded. "Dinnae mind the sheep. 'Tis public pasture land, though the beasties might try tae argue otherwise."

Bree looked at the hill and the old man standing at its summit, then turned back to her kinswoman. Puzzled, she shook her head.

"Ye can text me when ye've finished here. After that climb, and wha'ever the Old Man has tae say tae ye, ye'll no be wanting to walk the three miles to Heather House."

Bree looked out the window. She could see him more clearly now, shining with the opalescent light of the Otherworld. He stood, his oaken staff spiraling out of the earth and grey hair and beard billowing with his kilt in the breeze. His slate grey eyes opened before her and Bree's breath caught in her throat.

"On ye go, now." Caitlìn prompted. "Dinnae keep the Old Man waiting."

15

Bree heard the gravel churn from the pullout several feet below. Pausing her climb up Dunvegan tor to look behind her, she watched the Land Rover merge onto the roadway and disappear around the corner as Caitlìn headed back through the village.

She frowned, her gaze lingering where she lost sight of the truck. *Maybe I should have gone with her. We have so little time together before she leaves.*

"Remember who you are, chiya," the voice of her Bear Ally whispered through her. *"Remember and discover the Truth hidden within you."*

Bree turned forward, prepared to welcome her Ally. Instead, she found herself face to face with a rather determined looking sheep. He stood a few feet above her, his front hooves planted on a natural outcropping of the hill. Bree could see others of his kith and kin cowering several feet behind him in twos and threes. As one of the back-standers brayed nervously, the lead sheep stamped his hoof upon the earth, jutted his chin and grunted.

"You must be the chief," Bree mused aloud. Bowing her head she added, "Peace be upon you, Blessed One, and Peace be between us." She lifted her head. "Respectfully, I beg your leave to pass."

The sheep stared at her and held his ground. Behind him, the others stood stark still, their bodies tensed. A shrill chatter nipped at Bree's awareness.

"I mean you no harm." Bree lifted her right hand and placed it upon her heart for emphasis. The movement flashed through the crowd of sheep. In silent alarm, the animals bounded in all directions, their tails flailing behind them.

Bree chuckled loudly, her hand slipping back to her side. Shaking her head, she continued up the hill. With each step, the sheep bleated their disapproval at her. The chief of the herd ran toward her and, remaining well out of arm's reach, grunted loudly. Bree stopped, stared and grunted in return. The sheep bounded downhill, his herd crying loudly after him.

"I did ask politely," she called after the retreating sheep. "And it is public pasture, after all."

"*Crrruck!*"

Bree lifted her face skyward. Overhead, her Raven Ally flew into view. She watched the midnight black wings pump their way up the hill. Stretching to glide upon invisible thermals, her Ally spiraled to land upon the single monolith, standing tall and silent at the top of the hill. As her eyes tracked down the rough, three-meter length of the stone, the grey eyes of the old man snapped into view.

He leaned against the staff he held in his left hand and beckoned her with the right. *"Come."*

Gaze locked with his, she climbed to the top of the hill. Standing before him, she bowed. "Peace be upon you, Ancient One." She paused, head lowered, awaiting his reply.

"And upon you."

Bree lifted her gaze. The slate grey eyes blazed with opalescent light. They shimmered, spilling a cascade of images through her too fast for her to track. She trusted she would be able to recall them when the time was right.

She lifted her right hand and placed it over her heart. "Peace be between us..."

The Old Man drew his staff over his heart. *"... now and through all time."*

Light gleamed from his eyes and poured through Bree. She drank it in, let it fill her awareness to overflowing, then closed her eyes. Breathing deeply, she drew the light to the very edges of her energetic body. Still resting on her chest, her hand tingled as a heartbeat pulsed through her. It resounded within her, below her, above her. In her inner vision, she could see the light gleaming more brightly with each throbbing beat.

"Why come Ye to this place, Raven Child?"

Bree sighed. She knew the answer. It ached within her, waiting for her to acknowledge it and embrace the Truth. But to speak it, she knew, meant accepting it fully with no going back. Opening her eyes, she lowered her gaze to the ground. *Am I really ready?*

"Trust," Gwen's voice urged from the Otherworld. *"Trust in Love again."*

She raised her eyes to meet those of the Old Man. He stood waiting, his grey beard and hair drifting on the breeze. His question echoed around her, whispered from the earth and waters. *"Why come Ye to this place, Raven Child?"*

The words rose up and out of her, bubbling softly like the waters of a spring. "To find my way back to the living."

"To embrace the living, you must first let go of the dead."

Bree considered his words in silence, her black hair billowing around her in the breeze. "How?"

The Old Man lifted his right hand and pointed. Bree let her gaze track the length of that hand, following it like a sight across the waters of the loch to a local mountain. Rising and rolling in a series of hills, the earth stretched to reveal the contours of a sleeping woman. Eyes closed, the face turned slightly away from Bree. She could hear the woman sighing, could see her hair drifting with the heather in the breeze.

"She is the Mother of this land. Go to Her, Raven Child. She waits to show you the way."

Firelight twinkled on the horizon, drawing Bree's gaze. Were those torches burning atop that mountain?

Warmth spread slowly through her chest. She looked down and discovered the right hand of the Old Man now rested upon her. A soothing balm, the tenderness of his touch seeped into her, and she let herself drink it in. Lifting her gaze, the slate grey of his eyes filled her view and she smiled.

Light blazed through her awareness. Brilliant and stark, it seared across her forehead, blinding her. Gasping, she closed her eyes against the glare. Hot, white light pierced through her and she panted harshly. Sliding from the inner corner of her left eyebrow to the right, the light arched downward, passed just above the bridge of her nose, and curved back upward to hover above the inner corner of her right eyebrow. With a flash, it arched slowly downward again, this time passing well above the bridge of her nose as it seared a line on its way back to her left eyebrow. The outline complete, the image of a crescent flamed again through Bree's inner vision.

"Go in Peace, Raven Child." The Old Man's voice shimmered through her, twinkling with the soft sigh of silver bells. *"Go with my blessing, Bree MacLeod, and with the blessing of the Sìdhe. And remember, Child of the Sìdhe... We are still here."*

White light flashed and raced through her in a heartbeat. Then, just as quickly, it was gone. Blinking to restore her vision, Bree glanced into emptiness. She pivoted and circled, but saw no one. The Old Man was gone. Only the stone remained beside her, quiet and watchful on the hill. As her vision cleared, she gazed across the waters of the loch to the Mother Mountain. Torchlight clearly flickered across the top of MacLeod's Tables.

She shivered. Her legs trembled and she placed her right hand upon the stone to steady herself. A gentle hum rose to kiss her fingers in greeting. It stretched up her arm and spilled strength into her. Leaning her forehead against the ancient rock, she exhaled.

"Thank you, Ancient One. Blessed is the Mystery."

16

Bree checked her telephone. No new messages. She had texted Caitlìn on her way down the hill but so far, no response. *Maybe it didn't send?* She scrolled through her messages and tapped open the thread with her kinswoman. The word *sent* was stamped clearly beneath her recent entry. With a shrug, Bree returned the telephone to her pocket. Leaning back against a large boulder at the edge of the pullout, she settled in to wait for the promised ride back to Heather House.

Her forehead throbbed in the cool evening air. Closing her eyes, she lifted tentative fingertips to her aching skin. A thin line burned under her touch as she traced the welt the Guardian had etched anew upon her brow. Sliding her fingers along the arching lines, the image of a shining crescent filled her awareness.

Bree dropped her hand to her side and sighed. *First Brìghid, now the Old Man.*

"It will burn until you embrace it fully." The voice of Mother Brìghid echoed through her.

Why? Bree shook her head. *What does it mean?*

The shrill sound of metal sliding against metal cut through her. Eyes snapping open, Bree pushed herself off the boulder. Her body tensed as, by instinct, her feet sought level ground. Ready for a fight, she turned toward the sound.

A flash of blue drew her gaze as the front end of a pickup truck popped into view. Its brakes shrieked in complaint as it stopped at the intersection opposite the hill. Watching it turn toward her onto the A850, Bree could see the body was covered in mud. She exhaled hard and chuckled. *Someone's been having some fun.* Grinning, she relaxed and leaned back against the boulder.

Bree watched the pickup gain some speed then slow its approach. As it turned left into the pullout directly in front of her, she scanned the interior. A smile lit the face of the driver, a young man whose curly brown hair spilled out from under a green, knitted cap. Bree saw his smile widen as he caught sight of her. With a quick wave, he climbed out of the pickup and closed the driver's side door.

"Hullo, Bree MacLeod!"

Bree furrowed her brow. "Have we met?"

The man chuckled. "No." He stepped toward her, hand extended. "Hamish MacSween."

Bree looked at the open hand and wondered if she should take it. Narrowing her eyes, she studied the man before her. His work kilt swayed above mud-dusted shins that disappeared into woolen socks and well-worn, ankle-high walking boots. The sleeves of a wool sweater, the same color green as his hat, were pushed up to his elbows, revealing strong, muscular arms and hands. As the soft, earthy scent of pinesap filled her nose, Bree stifled a desire to reach out and touch him.

The man shifted his hands to his hips and rocked back onto his heels. Bree tried not to notice the muscular knees peeking out from under his swaying kilt as a fresh smile lit up his face. "Caitlìn sent me."

Bree shook her head. *This isn't the city*, she chided herself. Stepping forward, she extended her hand to meet his. "Sorry," she nodded. "*Is deas bualadh leat*... Lovely to meet you."

Hamish's eyes beamed. "Ye have the Gaelic!"

"Well," Bree shrugged. "I am learning. Irish I have, but Scots is a wee bit different."

He released her hand and returned his to his hips. "Ach, well, 'tis always a pleasure tae hear the language. Een more so on the tongue of such a lovely lass."

His eyes twinkled as they held Bree's gaze. Heat flamed across her face and she realized, too late, she was blushing. Dropping her chin, she let her dark hair fall to conceal her face. "You are too kind."

Fire seared up her legs and spread across her torso. Lifting her gaze, Bree realized it was her turn to be studied. Deep, brown eyes raked up the length of her then locked with hers. As the world slowed around her, a heartbeat filled her ears.

"Tha bròn orm... I'm sorry..." The clansman's voice echoed from the Otherworld.

Goddess bumps shivered across her skin and Bree shook her head, breaking the connection. "You said Caitlìn sent you?"

"Aye." Hamish nodded. "She said ye needed carrying, tae Heather House." He bowed, his work kilt shimmying, then stepped back and gestured to the pickup. "M'lady."

His eyes twinkled. When he winked suddenly, Bree laughed despite herself. Walking behind him toward the mud-covered truck, she wondered what the Old Man would think of this mischievous laddie. She glanced up the hill but saw only the stone, watchful and quiet.

Hamish opened the passenger door and Bree climbed inside. She watched him cross in front of the pickup, open the door and settle himself into the driver's seat. With a quick grin, he started the engine and put the truck into gear. As he steered the pickup back onto the A850, she saw him nod toward the hill.

"Was it worth it?'

Bree frowned and shook her head. "Sorry?"

"The view. From the stone. Was it worth the climb?" He gestured toward the hill. The brakes shrieked as he slowed to turn the pickup onto the A863 into Dunvegan Village, and Bree shivered.

"Oh. Yes." Bree nodded, grasping the strap above the window to steady herself through the turn. "Very much so."

Slate grey eyes blazed in her inner vision as the voice of the Old Man echoed through her. "*We are still here.*"

The pickup cleared the village and the Mother Mountain rose into view, still sleeping in her hillside across the loch. Bree opened her mouth and drew breath to speak, then hesitated.

She considered the man from the corner of her eyes. His energy shone brilliant and bright as starlight, radiating with the deep clarity of peace. *Is he one of us? Another child of the Sídhe?* She wondered. His radiant presence might reflect an active relationship with the People of Peace, the Fae, as The Old Ones were often called. *If not, would he understand?*

She shifted her gaze to view him more fully. She saw the muscles in his thighs bunch under his well-worn kilt as he engaged the clutch and shifted gears. Dried mud marked the stick shift with his broad fingerprints. The husky scent of pinesap wafted across her and she drew a deep breath. *Maybe his inner brilliance is borne of a life lived outdoors?*

She knew Otherworldly vision, or what the locals called the Second Sight, was commonly accepted in Scotland. But *the Sídhe* were another matter. While the locals would certainly acknowledge their presence, not everyone considered the Ancient Race benevolent or even peaceful, despite their Gaelic name.

Probably best not to risk offending him. She looked away. She would have to ask her kinswoman just how far she could trust this cheerful laddie.

Caitlin. The image of her friend rose in her inner vision. *Why didn't she come herself?* Bree turned toward Hamish. "Is everything okay? With Caitlìn, I mean."

He chuckled. "That lass has her hands full, to be sure." He glanced at her and held her gaze just long enough for heat to burn across her face before returning his eyes to the road. "A houseful of punters stepped into her bonnie den just as her phone chimed. So happens I was there—we were discussing her trip to Inverness Airport tomorrow." He shrugged. "She could nay leave a full house, so I offered to come meself and carry ye."

Bree frowned. "I thought she wasn't taking in guests tonight."

"She did nay plan to, until the lot arrived." He beamed in her direction. "She could hardly say no tae them once they were in the door."

"Fàilte abhaile...welcome home..." A woman's voice whispered through her. Eyes, soft and pale as moonlight, sparkled in her inner awareness as a smile glowed to life, then burst into cascading radiance. Bree watched the silvery bits dissolve and wondered, was the welcome meant for the guests or for herself?

Sunlight flashed off the waters of the loch. Bree followed the blaze as it bathed the Mother Mountain in radiance. Letting her gaze track up the side of the mountain, she saw torchlight flash across the top of MacLeod's Tables.

"She is the Mother of this land. Go to Her, Raven Child. She waits to show you the way."

I'm coming, Bree whispered silently. *Please wait for me.*

As the pickup slowed, the wail of metal upon metal cut through her again and Bree shivered. She turned in time to see Hamish steer the truck left onto the gravel driveway of Heather House and park beside Caitlìn's Land Rover. Bree slid out of the truck and Hamish caught up with her on the walk to the front door. With a grin, he opened the door and followed her into the foyer.

17

A flood of women's voices washed over Bree as she stepped into Heather House. Cascading from all directions, the flow rocked her and she stumbled. Forcing her awareness into her feet, she breathed in the solidity of the tile floor beneath her until she found her balance again. As the next wave of bubbling laughter poured over Bree, she tracked the current to the stairs in front of her. There, two women stood on different steps facing each other, their arms wrapped around each other's shoulders. Bree watched their cheeks touch in a ritual of welcoming. With each smile, golden light streamed through the foyer.

Another wave pulsed through the vestibule as a third woman dashed around the corner from the den. As Bree swayed with the tide, the woman on the uppermost step spread her arms wide and shrieked gleefully. Golden brilliance flashed between the friends, and the newcomer ran up the stairs as the loving dance of welcome enfolded all three.

Bree stood in the entryway, bathed in that golden radiance. It pulsated all around her, echoing off the walls of Heather House. As it slowly seeped into her, an ache spilled through her, spreading in its wake a warmth from heart to limbs. As the pulsation deepened into a heartbeat, a smile stretched through

Bree and illuminated her face. Awash in the shimmering radiance, a single word filled her awareness. *Belonging.*

"Bree, you're back!" Tracking the familiar voice, Bree turned to see Caitlìn appear out of the den. Her friend gracefully balanced a stack of clean, heather- and sage-colored bath towels in her arms. "Hamish, thanks for fetching her."

"*Thà fàilte romhat...* You're welcome, lass!" He took two steps toward Caitlìn, arms extended. "May I carry those for ye?"

With a laugh, Caitlìn pulled her arms out of his reach and headed toward the now-empty steps. "Ach, no! I can manage. Just make yourselves comfortable." She nodded toward the den and started up the stairs.

Hamish stood on the bottom step, arms raised protectively. Bree noticed his eyes followed Caitlìn on her journey up the stairs, as if he were assisting her with her burden from afar. She smiled to herself, grateful her kinswoman had found such a caring friend.

Caitlìn disappeared down the upstairs hall and, sighing noisily, Hamish dropped his hands to his sides. Shaking his head, he glanced once more up the stairs, then turned to face Bree. "C'mon," he gestured. "The den is this way."

A fire burned in the grate, warming the cozy room. Grateful to be off her feet, Bree sank into the overstuffed sofa closest to the fireplace. Closing her eyes, she leaned back into the soft warmth and let herself drift. Echoes of the day whispered around her in dissolving snippets. Then Hamish's voice rose clear and firm out of her memory...*"So happens I was there—we were discussing her trip to Inverness Airport tomorrow."*

Bree opened her eyes and looked around the room. Hamish lounged on the arm of the sofa to her right. Gazing steadily into the fire, he leaned forward and grabbed an apple from the bowl on the table in front of them. She watched as he bit into the apple, then shook her head.

"Wait," she started. "I had planned to drive Caitlìn to the airport tomorrow."

Releasing his gaze from the fire, Hamish faced her and spoke through a full mouth. "Aye, ye had. But ye canno leave a houseful of lassies. No doubt they'll be wanting their breakfast."

She chuckled. "No doubt."

Hamish swallowed the mouthful of apple. "And, helpful though I can be, in the kitchen I'm a disaster." He shook his head, ruefully. "I can snake a drain, clean a mean sheet, even fold a neat bed. But I burn everything in a pan. So, breakfast is up to you."

Bree laughed. "I'll keep that in mind."

Deep, brown eyes locked with hers. Holding her gaze, his eyes sparkled, sending warmth to flood through her.

"I hope ye do."

18

Quiet finally settled through Heather House. Walking past Caitlìn's bedroom, Bree was glad to see no light spilled from under the door. Despite her friend's protests, Bree had insisted Caitlìn retire to her bedroom to finishing packing and go to bed. In the end, Hamish had sided with Bree and escorted Caitlìn out of the kitchen and down the hall. Seeing the light was off, Bree smiled, grateful her kinswoman would get some rest before her early departure the next morning.

Bree herself had finished in the kitchen preparing breakfast for the guests. She had squeezed fresh orange juice, pulled blood pudding out of the freezer to defrost and whipped the egg and vanilla marinade for tomorrow's French toast. As Bree laid the silverware and chargers on the tables, something had shifted. A mantle of power had draped across her shoulders and she knew the guardianship of Heather House—if only temporarily—had transferred to her.

She stepped into the downstairs guest room. The smallest in the house, she and Caitlìn had agreed the room should be hers for the duration of her stay. At first, Bree had objected. She could easily stay in Caitlìn's room and keep the extra bed available for guests. But Caitlìn had insisted. At the very least, her friend had argued, Bree deserved a place of refuge, no matter how small.

Tonight Bree was grateful for the privacy. Pulling the door closed behind her, she stood in the middle of the room, closed her eyes and exhaled. With each breath, she let it all go—the noise of the day, the thoughts and emotions lingering from her encounter with Màire, the echoes of her bantering with Hamish. Anything other than her own life force, she let it fall away. Softly shaking her fingers, she released the residual energies back to the earth, back to the Mother, to the great cauldron of Life.

Slowly, a gleam of clarity blossomed to shine within her and Bree turned her focus to her own vibration. Her heartbeat called to her. Steady and even, she allowed herself to sink into that rhythm. On and on the pulsation flowed, filling Bree with its constant affirmation of life. *"I am,"* it whispered. *"I am... I am..."*

That gleam swelled to a blaze and she stood, breathing in her own light, her own lifeforce. A wave of gratitude for the blessings of the day rose up from her core and she let it wash through her. It spilled through her torso, down her legs and arms, and out her fingers and toes. Then it rippled out into the world around her. Flowing into This World and the Otherworld, it shimmered with the gentle tinkling of silver bells.

"We are still here..."

The voice of the Old Man echoed through her and Bree opened her eyes. Moonlight flooded through the window into her room and enfolded her in a silvery-white halo. Tiny motes of light sparkled and danced, swirling around her. Casting her gaze to trace the streaming rays out the window, she gasped.

Torchlight flickered, golden and beckoning, atop the Mother Mountain.

"We are still here..."

A pounding filled her awareness. *Are those drums?* The throbbing rhythm stretched and blurred, releasing a heartbeat that pulsed through her. Silvery-white light erupted from beneath her feet and poured to her very edges. With each pulsation, the light glowed brighter and brighter, until it flashed into a blaze. As her world blanched around her, Bree closed her eyes and slipped through the whiteness into the Otherworld.

19

Hair loose and billowing in the breeze, Bree walks with bare feet upon heather-covered earth. Torchlight blazes all around her and she shivers in her chemise. She is not alone. Just beyond the flames, people are moving, drifting in the rippling shadows. She stretches her neck to see who is there. But the firelight blazes, blurring her view, and she shields her face from the glare.

"Come. She is waiting for you."

The Old Man stands before her, his right hand extended toward her. Raven sits perched upon his left shoulder, torch fire dancing in her black eyes. With a nod from her Ally, Bree reaches through the flickering light and takes his hand.

Drums pound all around her. The relentless rhythm pummels her and she cringes. Gasping for air, she struggles to catch her breath.

The scream of metal upon metal wails through her and she shivers. The hilt of her sword presses cold in her grip as she cuts and parries blade after blade. She pants, unable to stop yet unable to win clear. Shaking sweat from her eyes, she cries out.

"I don't understand!"

A hand falls hard upon her left shoulder and pushes her into a spin. Lost in the blurring of darkness and torchlight, she loses her balance and falls toward the ground.

．　．　．

Bree's body jerked. Her eyes snapped open, and she stared into her room at Heather House. The moonlight gone, she stood now in darkness. Panting softly, she trembled as a cold sweat chilled her body.

"I don't understand," she muttered.

Her body shook. Stumbling through the unfamiliar darkness, she fell onto the bed, pulled the quilt over her head and surrendered to sleep.

20

"So, how's it going?" Warm and resonant, the energetic presence of Fergus Sinclair reached through the telephone and wrapped around Bree. She smiled at the touch. It seemed like ages since she had heard a familiar voice.

"Well, I've texted Caitlìn only six or seven times. For the first two weeks, I'd call that a success."

Two weeks, she marveled as Fergus' soft chuckle drifted in the background. *Has it only been two weeks?* Since Caitlìn left for Cape Breton, Bree's days were a blur. Flowing from kitchen to foyer to laundry room to bedrooms to foyer to kitchen again, she never stopped. *How has Caitlìn managed for two years on her own?*

Bree stepped into the den. Sunlight sparkled off the waters of the loch, illuminating the hill the locals called MacLeod's Tables. Drawn toward the view, Bree paused in front of the large bay window.

Slate grey eyes flashed in her inner vision and Bree frowned. What was it the Old Man had called this mountain? She closed her eyes and listened as his voice rose again within her.

"She is the Mother of this land. Go to Her, Raven Child. She waits to show you the way."

She opened her eyes. Torchlight shimmered on the top of the mountain. Bree narrowed her eyes as her inner vision engaged. *Are those women?* Spiraling across the flat surface of the summit, Bree could clearly see them. Hair flying loose down their backs and long skirts billowing, they held their fiery torches high as they danced.

But, how? Who are they? Bree wondered.

The line of women wound its way across the summit. As the fiery glow snaked onward, one woman stepped out of the undulating dance and turned suddenly toward Bree. Her eyes glinting brightly in the light of her torch, the woman walked to the edge of the hill and stood facing Bree. Something touched Bree's consciousness... a wisp of light... a gentle pressure... the soft whisper of awareness.

"She is waiting for you." The voice of her Raven Ally rippled through Bree as the woman's eyes flashed.

I'm coming, Bree called silently.

"Did Caitlin say when she would be back?"

Bree looked to her left, toward the sound of Fergus' voice. The telephone pressed against her ear and she chuckled. She had forgotten about their conversation. She glanced back toward the Mother Mountain, but the dancers and their torches were gone.

"Bree?" Fergus prompted her.

"Sorry..." Bree placed her right hand over her eyes and shook her head to clear it. "Not specifically. She said she'd like to stay for a month or so. I told her not to hurry." The warning bell chimed on the dryer, alerting her the sheets were almost ready, and Bree groaned inwardly. "After just two weeks of running the bed and breakfast, I am certain she could use the holiday."

Fergus sighed. "It's that busy?"

Bree could hear his disappointment. Like the keening of a stream across stones, it spilled through her awareness. "It is. The weekends book solid in advance and the weekdays always seem to fill. A day can begin with only a single bed reserved but by nightfall, the house is full."

Light glowed in Bree's inner vision. Soft and pale as moonlight, it swirled to reveal the face of a woman. Radiant hair cascaded free beyond the woman's shoulders and her eyes sparkled as a smile glowed to life. A throaty laugh caressed Bree as she watched the woman, ghostly and shimmering, wave traveler after traveler into Heather House.

"Fàilte abhaile...welcome home..." the woman whispered to their souls.

Bree shifted her right hand to rest upon her heart. *Blessed is the Mystery.*

The sound of water rippling washed over her as Fergus sighed. Opening her eyes, she walked away from the window. "How is life in Saint Louis?"

"Quiet." He paused. "Everyone keeps asking about you."

"Everyone?" Bree frowned. While she knew she was well respected in her adopted city, she doubted she was missed.

"I was at the café yesterday."

That explains it. Bree nodded to herself as she sat on the arm of the sofa. "And how are things there?"

"Sheila has the place well in hand."

"She always does."

Bree traced the ribbing on the lavender throw pillows with her finger. The lines ran straight and narrow, like the floorboards of Café de Lys. She could see the café, flooded with sunlight streaming through the floor-to-ceiling windows and filled with laughter. Gwen's laughter. Bree could still hear it echoing off the café walls, wild and rumbling like summer thunder.

The café had been Gwen's first love. How many times had Bree driven by that place, telling herself she should stop and enjoy a cuppa? She still remembered the day she finally did stop. The fleur-de-lys on the front window had filled her vision until she pulled over and parked the car. Looking back, she wondered—as she reached for the door that day, did she know her life would never be the same?

The chime on the dryer sounded and Bree sighed. "That's the dryer. Time to fold sheets and make beds before the afternoon arrivals."

"Okay. I'll let you go. But..." Fergus' voice wavered.

"But what?"

"I could come and help you. For a while. If you'd like."

Bree shivered. "Thanks, Fergus. That's really kind, truly. But, I'm okay for now."

Bree placed the basket of freshly dried sheets on the coffee table in the center of the den. Grateful for a few moments of quiet, she stood facing the large bay window. Late afternoon sunlight streamed through the glass, bathing her and the room in golden warmth.

She pulled a flat sheet from the basket and started folding. As her hands guided themselves through the familiar process, the closing words of her conversation with Fergus drifted into her mind.

"I could come and help you. For a while. If you'd like."

Bree frowned. *Why am I pushing him away?*

Fergus Sinclair was one of her closest friends. She had known him for years and had spent hours alone with him, contemplating the details of their lives and spiritual experiences. A fellow mystic, his soulful, heart-centered vision of living was the closest she had found to her own family tradition. Conversations with him always brought her home to her own practices. She knew she could confide in him. More than that, she trusted him.

But things are different now.

Bree stood up straight. The partially folded sheet sagged, suspended between her hands. Had their relationship really changed since Gwen's death? Was Fergus any less a friend than he had been before? She completed the final fold of the sheet, then drew it close to her chest. *If Gwen were still alive, would I have hesitated? Or would I have told him to come?*

She placed the folded sheet on the overstuffed sofa in front of her and pulled the next sheet from the basket. Her gaze drifted through the window, beyond Loch Dunvegan and the Mother Mountain, into the past.

Firelight had danced across Fergus' face. "You are fortunate, Bree. You have a legal right to return. But what about the rest of us?"

She had joined him that night in Forest Park for the annual calling of the clans, a Celtic Heritage event sponsored by the Caledonian Society of Saint Louis. Fergus carried the torch for Clan Sinclair that year, while Bree lit the ceremonial bonfire in the name of Clan MacLeod. She had just returned from one of her extended visits to Ireland. Standing with Fergus beside the bonfire after the ceremony, she considered living permanently in Kildare, in the cottage she had inherited there.

Fergus nodded as he reminded her, she had a legal connection to the Isle of Éireann through her mother. And, as a property owner, she had the right and the means to return. Fergus, she knew, was not so fortunate. His name was the only traceable connection to his ancestral home in Rossyln, Scotland. With no legal right to stay, he could visit Scotland for three months before the law required him to leave.

She could still see the sorrow, spilling across his face with the shadows as the firelight shifted in the breeze. "What about the rest of us? What about those of us who live in exile and long to return? Those whose hearts and souls yearn to live on home soil, whose bodies ache for the pulsation of that land, whose blood cries for the song of home, but who have no legal means to return?"

Staring out the window of Heather House, Bree set the folded sheet on the sofa. He was right, she realized. So many still lived in exile.

Firelight blazed all around her, filling her inner vision. Just beyond the flames, she saw people moving, drifting in the rippling shadows. One by one, she watched them approach, stare through sad eyes into the fire, then drift back to the shadows.

Another woman approached the fire. Bree stretched her arms toward the woman but her hands passed right through the form. Slowly dissolving to shadow, the woman turned and reached for Bree. Then she and the fire were gone.

Bree stood in the den of Heather House, a tear spilling down her cheek. As her arms sank back to her sides, she wondered. "What about those who cannot get home?"

22

Bree closed her eyes and shuddered. *Where did that come from?* Opening her eyes, she looked around the den of Heather House. Sunlight still streamed in through the bay window. The basket of freshly dried sheets sat on the table, half-full and waiting for her.

A fresh tear spilled down her cheek and Bree reached to wipe it away. "C'mon girl," she chattered to herself. "There's work to be done."

She shook herself and pulled another sheet out of the basket. As her hands again guided themselves through the familiar folding process, she gazed out the window at the Mother Mountain.

He's right, she thought. *What about the exiles—those who have gotten lost or had loss imposed upon them through an ancestor's choice to leave? What about those who cannot return or cannot find their way home?*

The air in the room thickened and everything slowed around her. She drew the folded sheet to her chest and stood motionless, sinking into the deepening stillness. Engaging her inner vision, she sent her awareness drifting through her body. Heat prickled along her back. Directing her focus into that warmth, she realized she was not alone. A dense presence pulsated directly behind her.

Her breath came hard and shallow. Moving very slowly, she dropped the folded sheet onto the sofa and pivoted carefully *deiseal*, turning sunwise in a physical prayer for life-affirming, co-creative flow. The light in the room shuddered and the sound of fire crackled in her ears. As her back reached the window, she stiffened.

A woman stood before her.

Long, black hair cascading unbound down her back, the woman watched quietly but with purpose. A thick cloak covered the woven plaid that spilled down her shoulders and flowed out from her waist to the floor. Three blue lines spiraled around her left eye and down the side of her throat to disappear under her plaid. Instinctively, Bree knew the lines continued down the left side of the woman's body all the way to her toes.

Power pulsated around her as sunlight spilled through the woman. Careful to remain motionless, Bree called to her Allies. *Is she a ghost?*

"Not exactly," the voice of her Raven Ally whispered from the Otherworld. *"Greet her, chiya. She has been waiting for you."*

For me? Why? Bree wondered.

When her Ally offered no further explanation, Bree opted for a traditional greeting. She placed her right hand over her heart and bowed her head to the woman. *"Síocháin duit...* Peace be upon you."

Fierce green eyes locked on Bree and the woman bowed her head in return. *"And upon Ye."* Lifting her head, the woman stepped closer and stared intently at Bree's face. *"Who are Ye?"*

Bree shifted her feet for a stronger stance and drew a long, slow breath. "I am Bree MacLeod, daughter of the goddess Brighid, and Child of the *Sídhe.*"

The woman's eyebrows pulsed, then returned to neutral, the intent expression on her face never wavering. Bree grounded her energy as the woman stepped close enough to raise her left hand and touch Bree's forehead.

Heat seared across her brow as the woman's finger tracked the welt between Bree's eyebrows. Opalescent light shimmered in Bree's inner vision, etching the path of the woman's touch and illuminating the image on her forehead. As the crescent blazed in its fullness, light blazed through Bree.

The woman stepped back and nodded slowly. Green eyes locked upon Bree, she whispered, *"Pàiste an Shìdhe... Child of the Sídhe..."*

Dissolving into the sunlight, the woman stretched her arms toward Bree, then she was gone.

23

"Thanks, Hamish." Bree smiled as she unpacked the bag of fresh meats and groceries Hamish picked up for her. "I never would have made it to Portree today."

"*Thà fàilte romhat...*" Hamish nodded. "Ye are welcome, lass."

Bree's forehead burned. Bending over the cloth bag, she resisted the urge to touch the thin welt she knew stretched between her eyebrows. Instead, she frowned. It had been days since her most recent encounter with the Old Man. Why was it bothering her now? *The woman with the blue spirals.* With the late arrival of an unexpected group of three guests to the inn last night, Bree had all but forgotten about yesterday afternoon's Otherworldly visitor. As her forehead pulsed, she wondered if Bríghid were prompting her to remember.

Hamish shook his head and chuckled. "And just how long did those lassies linger?"

Bree paused mid-reach into the cloth bag as her shoulders drooped. "One o'clock! They sat over their breakfast dishes sipping tea until just past noon. And it was one o'clock when they finally closed the door and departed." Bree pulled the paper-wrapped bundle of fresh blood pudding out of the bag and set it on the kitchen counter. "Luckily, I had enough time to clean and prep the rooms before the three o'clock arrivals."

"Well, ye managed it right enough, and I'd say your kinswoman could nay do better."

Bree folded the now-empty shopping bag and turned toward Hamish. His deep brown eyes twinkled at her as he leaned against the kitchen wall. Heat prickled under her skin, threatening to rise and color her face crimson. She shook her head, spilling her black hair to hide her face. "I don't know how Caitlìn manages it, day after day."

Hamish cocked his head. "Aye, ye do, lass. Ye've been managing just fine these past weeks. I know, 'cause I've been watching ye."

Red heat blazed across her cheeks. "*Tapadh leat...* Thank you, Hamish. But, I know you are just being kind."

"Ye'd make a fine innswoman, Bree MacLeod."

"What?" Bree looked him full in the face. The usual twinkle was gone from those dark eyes. Instead, they watched her, calm and serious. "Whatever do you mean?"

He leaned toward her. "I mean, lass, ye should consider staying on awhile, even making Heather House your home. T'would be easier, the two of ye managing the inn. T'is certain Caitlìn would be happy tae have ye. I know already how much she values ye as a friend."

Bree shook her head. "Hamish, I have no legal right to live or work in Scotland." The words were out of her mouth before she could consider them or their implications.

"But," he stepped toward her, "your name. Are ye no a MacLeod?"

"Of course." Bree placed the empty shopping bag in its bin on the shelf. Facing Hamish again, she shrugged. "But my father was born in Canada, as was his father before him. Here, like most places, a great-grand relation is too far removed to form a basis for residency or citizenship. And under European Union rules, Canadian citizens no longer have open access to work in the United Kingdom. So, I have the name but nothing more."

My name, she sighed inwardly. *It truly is all I have left.* Hadn't she spoken similar words to Mother Bríghid only a few weeks earlier?

Or could it be a sign of something more? She could see herself living again with her kinswoman, but move to Scotland? She had never even considered the idea. All her life, she had heard Ireland calling her. Had she been mistaken? Was her true destination a bit further north?

Hamish laughed. "Ach, dinnae ye worry. *That* is easy enough to resolve."

Bree stared at him. She trembled. *He couldn't possibly be suggesting...* Ice spilled through her body, rooting her where she stood. Only her heart moved, pounding through her like a drum. Cautiously, she took a breath. "Meaning what, exactly?"

His dark eyes stared back at her. "Ye make it legal for ye."

"And, how would I do that?"

A smile spread slowly across his face. "By marrying a local, of course."

Bree shivered. A frisson of terror shook loose from her core and rumbled through her. Bracing against the tremor, she closed her eyes.

Hamish continued, undaunted. "Sure, Caitlìn would have ye. The law here does allow for that, ye ken."

He paused and Bree opened her eyes. She drew breath to object—Caitlìn was her friend—but she could only stare.

Hamish stepped closer. "Now then, should ye prefer a different sort of option..." He stepped directly in front of her as he spoke, "... I might know of someone who could be interested."

He reached out and took her hand in his. Brown eyes locked upon hers, he lifted her hand to his lips and kissed it gently.

Bree's body shook. She fought to steady herself but failed. As he lowered her hand, Bree opened her mouth to speak. Her voice cracked. Pretending to cough, she cleared her throat. "But, Hamish, you hardly know me."

The familiar twinkle danced through his dark eyes. "Ach, well, we've two more months for that. But I've seen enough to be comfortable with giving things a try."

24

Bree sat on the edge of her bed surrounded in darkness. Moonlight spilled softly into the center of her snug room, illuminating a small circle. Like an Otherworldly nightlight come to comfort her.

He can't be serious.

Bree grabbed the edge of the bed to steady her trembling body. Marriage? The very idea was preposterous. Whether to a woman or a man—assuming Scottish law really allowed both options— she was still trying to get over Gwen. The thought of marrying someone, anyone, much less to remain in Scotland, was beyond consideration.

The light swirled in the center of her room, spiraling and dancing with an unseen tide. Her eyes tracked the flow as her mind raced.

Or was it?

Bree straightened. She had come to Scotland to help her kinswoman, that was certainly true. But what she had told the Old Man was true as well. She was here to find her way back to the living.

What if Scotland was her way back?

She frowned. She had never considered the possibility of

living in *Alba*, the land of her father's kin. Growing up with her mother's people, the Irish side of her relatives, it had always been Ireland. When she inherited her mother's cottage in Kildare, in Brighid's home county, her direction seemed clear. But, as she had reminded the Mother of her lineage only a few weeks ago, she was also a MacLeod.

What had Brighid said to her? *"It is time you learned your true connection to that name."* Bree shook her head. What did She mean?

"Exiles..." Màire's voice cut through her.

Was she one of the exiles? Her father's people had left Scotland three generations ago. Their legal connection to the land was broken, even though the traditions and the name continued.

Her heart pounded as her body trembled. *What if this is my place of belonging? What if this is the pathway home?*

The air in the room thickened and everything slowed around her. Her breath came hard and shallow while the light in the center of the room grew in intensity. Faster and faster it swirled and stretched upward toward the ceiling. Bree watched the dance, her body frozen to stillness on the side of the bed. Tendrils grew and intertwined before her eyes. As the light spilled back in upon itself, Bree watched threads of light weaving to create a form.

The woman with the blue spirals stood before her.

Long black hair cascaded unbound down her back as the woman bowed her head. *"Pàiste an Shìdhe... Child of the Sìdhe..."*

25

The woman stood quietly watching Bree, the yellow threads of her plaid gleaming in the moonlight. Bree's eyes tracked the folds of the cloth, so clear to her this time, up the woman's torso to the soft creases lining the ancient face. Bree had a sudden urge to reach out and touch the blue ink spiraling around the woman's left eye and snaking down her cheek and throat. She leaned forward on the bed, then hesitated. Instead, she sat back again, placed her right hand over her heart and bowed her head to the woman.

"*Síocháin duit...* Peace be upon you."

"*And upon Ye, Bree MacLeod.*"

The woman stepped forward and traced the welt on Bree's forehead with her left hand. Then she drew her hand over her heart. "*Ye are needed, Child of Peace.*"

Bree shifted her gaze to meet that of the woman. "Needed," she frowned. "How?"

"*To find the way back to living.*"

Bree shook her head. "I don't understand."

The woman held out her right hand to Bree. "*Come,*" she whispered. "*And I'll show Ye.*"

Bree looked around the room. She had not set a circle of protection around her that night, although she had set one for her general stay at Heather House. Was that enough to ensure her safe passage through whatever experience awaited her with this woman?

"Remember who you are..." The voice of her Bear Ally echoed through her.

Bree closed her eyes and called silently to the directions. *Peace be upon the Airds. Peace be in the North...* The air around her shifted. She paused, waiting until an energetic wall firmed behind her. *Peace be in the East...* She continued, drawing the protective circle *deiseal*, sunwise with the power of life-affirming creation. *Peace be in the South...* The energetic shield curved in front of her, enfolding her now. *Peace be in the West...* Holding her focus, she drew the shield back to north, to full circle. As the two ends connected, a ring of opalescent light blazed, surrounding her and the woman. *Peace be in the Center. Peace be in this journey. Peace be.*

Bree watched the final words of the ritual ripple through the newly-formed circle, sealing its edges with the blessing. Then a second ray of light shimmered around its perimeter, etching a silvery-blue ring of protection. Opening her eyes, Bree saw the woman's lips moving, echoing the final words of an encompassing.

Bree's eyes widened as her heart pounded. The woman had set the circle with her! Who was she? Setting her curiosity aside, Bree offered one more prayer. *Allies, be with me. Show me the way.*

The soft peal of silver bells spilled through the room. Spiraling around Bree, the song deepened as the voice of the Old Man washed through her. *"To embrace the living, you must first let go of the dead."*

Silvery light sparkled as the song curled around the woman's feet and ankles, then swirled slowly upward, spilling around her head and enfolding her shoulders in gentle radiance. Bree's eyes followed the shimmering dance as the soft lilt of the silver bells called her to the Otherside. Before her the woman waited, arm outstretched and bathed in the moonlight. Vision blurring, Bree reached and grasped the offered hand.

26

Fire blazes. Bree stands alone, black hair whipping a frenzy as the flames lash and encompass her. Crimson light flashes and the fire swallows her. It bursts through her feet and belly and races up her torso and limbs toward the night sky. Leaning into the uprush, Bree tilts her head back and marvels at the fiery dance. Consciously slowing her breath, she drinks in the power of the blaze with each inhale as she raises her eyes and open palms to the stars in honoring.

Her voice is a crackle within the flames. "Blessed is the Mystery."

In a sudden rush, the blaze exhales outward. Yawning in all directions, the flames stretch to form a sea of fire around her. A vast, undulating ring, the crimson-orange waters roil. Bree stands at the center, an island, separate from, yet at the very heart of the burning. Black hair lashing her face, she raises her hands to her sides. No wind buffets her skin, yet the frenzy around her wails. Watching the lava-like torrent race wider, her world falls silent.

Flames lick and rupture the far edge. Thin rivulets of fire pour into the darkness. Like Otherworldly solar flares, they stretch out of the undulating sea and reach in all directions. From the center, Bree watches the crimson-orange flares spill through the silence, then arch slowly sunwise. Spiraling in upon themselves, they stream tighter and tighter.

As the blazing coils collapse inward, myriad flash points streak through a night sky.

Bree stands surrounded by bonfires. As they drift closer, they rise to her eye level. Beneath the flickering, shadows stir within the darkness. An eerie rustling fills her awareness and the hairs rise on the back of her neck. Her breath comes short and shallow and she pivots, turning slowly, alone, at the center of the circle. Body tensed, she spreads her hands wide at her sides and opens her palms to the earth, affirming her peaceful intent. All around her, the shades continue their approach.

"Allies, be with me," she whispers.

As one, the fires flare to full flame, illuminating the circle. Everywhere Bree looks, eyes glitter in the flickering light. She turns more slowly now, her own eyes tracing the subtle outlines. Women and men stand all around her, each holding a blazing torch overhead. While their faces and clothing dissolve into the shadows, Bree realizes, their eyes are firmly focused on her.

"Crrruck!"

Bree lifts her gaze skyward. Above her a familiar shape races through the darkness. Wings stretching midnight-black against the currents, her Raven Ally glides through the night sky. As their eyes meet, her awareness locks with that of her Raven Ally and she is flying. Her arms stretch taut against the currents as her body leans, pressing in a spiral downward, downward, downward. Talons open and ready, she lands.

A prickling stings her left shoulder and Bree gasps. Her awareness again her own, she turns her head to the left and stares into the eye of her Raven Ally. She pulls her head out of the way as Raven shakes herself, draws her feathers around her and settles in dignified poise.

Bree exhales with relief. "Hello, Raven."

Raven tilts her head, locking a black eye with Bree's. "Hello, Raven Child." With a nod toward the others, her Ally whispers, "You are needed, Child of the Sidhe."

An eerie rustling wails and trembles through the encircling shadows, then dies suddenly. Bree shifts her gaze toward the silence. A shape shivers in the darkness. As it moves into the center of the circle, the form bends and shudders. In a blaze of light, the woman from her earlier encounter stands before Bree, torch held high. The woman bows her head.

"Sìochan duit... Peace be upon Ye." The voices around her intone their welcome.

"Sìochan duit... Peace be upon Ye," the woman echoes.

Bree bows in return, keeping her torso steady for Raven. "Agus síochan doibh... And upon you."

The woman raises her head and smiles. "Be Ye welcome as a guest to our circle, Bree MacLeod, Child of the Sìdhe. Know Ye—no harm shall come to Ye amongst us, now nor when Ye choose to depart. Nor do we claim any right of demand. We ask only that Ye listen and consider."

Bree's body tenses. Uncertain, she glances toward her Ally. A subtle nod fills her view.

She looks again around the circle. Faces obscured by the dancing firelight, she perceives only shapes, outlines of forms. Wherever she focuses her gaze, the images dissolve from her view even as the sense of presence remains. Letting her eyes drift unfocused through the flickering light, shadowy forms solidify in her peripheral view.

She faces the woman before her. "Who are you and what exactly is this place?"

"I am Britomaris." The woman gestures to the circle around her. "These are my people, my community of blood. And this is our exile."

27

"Exile?" Bree repeats the word, wondering if she heard correctly.

Britomaris nods slowly as shadows drift across her face.

Voices whisper through Bree's awareness. Snapshots of images rifle too fast for her to see, while begging her to witness them. She reaches for one. Metal glints in sunlight and blood pools on moss-covered earth. She tries to focus, to hold the image, but it wails in defiance and wriggles out of her grasp. Her vision spins and she pants from the effort. Closing her eyes, she shakes her head, trying to disrupt the flow. "But, how? Why? Who exiled you here?"

The torchfires sputter a haunting counterpoint to Britomaris' voice. "We dinnae ken."

Bree opens her eyes and meets those of the woman. "What do you mean, you don't know?"

Britomaris stands before Bree but says nothing. Bree looks around the circle at the eyes glittering in the darkness. From the corner of her own eyes she can almost see the people standing around her. Woven cloaks and leather greaves coalesce out of the shadows, then disappear as Bree turns to look at them directly. Only the eyes remain.

She shakes her head. "Raven, who are they? And what happened here?"

Raven tilts her head. "They were your kith and kin."

Firelight dances in the eyes of her Ally. Around her, the shadows recede slightly. From the corners of her eyes, Bree sees folds in clothes, leather wrappings around feet and legs, dim colors whispering out of the darkness. She turns her head to look at the man to her right. For a moment, for one beat of her heart, she can almost see him—raven-black hair above a green woolen cloak—before the darkness reclaims him.

She shakes her head. "I don't understand."

Bree turns back to the center of the circle and finds herself face to face with Britomaris. Brownish-green light trembles in the woman's eyes. Bree's breath catches in her throat and she hesitates. She wants to step back, to open the space between herself and Britomaris, but her body refuses. Instead, she shifts her gaze. The blue ink spiraling down the left side of the woman's face gleams and undulates.

"Trust..." Britomaris whispers as she presses her forehead to Bree's. Blue light blazes, cascading through Bree. She gasps, and the blue undulates, then spills into silver.

"We were happy here." Britomaris' voice throbs through her. Colors bleed out of the silver. Slowly, they seep across her vision, staining her view. Images rise out of the patchwork... A ring of thatched, stone roundhouses stretches from loch into tree line, an open-pit bonfire burning at its center... a group of people, smiling and lounging at ease, share a meal around the bonfire... people drift in dugouts, lines cast into the water.

"The land welcomed us, and we lived easy upon her." Britomaris' voice ripples the images, blurring the colors. New images rise into Bree's view... Another ring of thatched roundhouses. Smaller than the previous one, this ring nestles fully within a circle of trees... A circle of nine people enfolds two others in the center. One, dressed head to toe in black feathers, smears an ointment across the chest of the other, streaking the skin blue.

"We lived, two circles united in Oneness. The Sacred, the Mundane and the Mystery." Bree gasps as the image of a single circle arises before her. People stand, arms outstretched and fingers touching, as they dance in celebration around a central fire, encompassed in a circle of trees. Something soft brushes her fingertips.

"We were happy here."

Colors blur and spill across her vision, then coalesce to birth another image. A group of nine people lounge within the forest, sharing food and water. One man's skin glints blue in the dappled light. A set of antlers rests on the ground beside him. "We were deep in the heart of the sacred wood, honoring the Thrumming, the Wild Rushing of Life, keeping the Sacred Balance as those before us. The Running completed, we lingered for a meal." Britomaris' voice wavers. "The Sacred whispered nothing, sent no vision nor kenning. T'was he saw it first." The man painted in blue rises slowly to his feet. Staring into the west, his eyes squint, then lift to the sky. "Smoke," he mutters. "Smoke from the shore."

Bree's heart pounds and her body tenses. Tree limbs dart and reach into her as the earth blurs beneath her. She realizes she is running. "No", she reminds herself. "This is a sending. I am standing in an Otherworldly circle. They are the ones running."

Thunder rolls through her, shaking the very air around her. It crashes, pounding rhythmically through the forest. "The drums..." The woman's voice trembles, sorrow spilling with every syllable. "They were our only warning."

Pain sears through Bree's shoulder and the world around her blurs as she falls. Her head rocks hard upon the earth. Metal glints in the sunlight and blood pools on moss-covered earth, then her world goes dark.

Blue light blazes as pressure builds upon her forehead. The moist heat of skin upon skin fills her awareness and she focuses on that sense of touch. As the pressure grows, she grabs hold of it mentally. Using it like an Otherworldly rope, she pulls herself toward the ache. Inch by inch, she reaches out of the light and into the pressure, until she falls into darkness.

Her body shaking, Bree opens her eyes. Britomaris' head still presses against her own, the blue ink shimmering brightly. Bree raises her arms and pushes away from the woman, breaking the connection. Gasping from the effort, her body sways.

"Grrrack!" Raven scolds, hopping and teetering on her left shoulder.

Tears spill down Bree's cheeks and she struggles to catch her breath. As she forces her body still, Raven settles.

"They slaughtered us." Britomaris' voice floods through Bree. "They offered no warning, no declaration of challenge, not even the time to

draw arms. They spilled our blood where we stood and left no one alive to tend the dead."

Bree faces Britomaris. In silent awe, she watches the blue light shimmering around the woman's left eye and cheek dim, darken and sink back to ink. She shakes her head. "What does this have to do with me?"

"Truly, can Ye nay remember?" Britomaris stands before Bree, sorrow filling her eyes. "Only one of the Ancient Blood, claimed and fully acknowledged, can help us journey home. Only one like you, Bree MacLeod."

The torchlight gutters and Britomaris glances around the circle. Stepping backward, she rejoins the others of her community. "Sure, there be reasons to help us and reasons to say nay. Consider our request well. We have waited so long for Ye, Child of the Sìdhe. We will be here as we have been, waiting."

The fires flicker once more, then die. As the eyes glittering around her fade, Bree sinks into darkness. "Who are they," she whispers to her Raven Ally. "Who are these exiles?"

"That, only the Old Man may tell you."

28

Bree paused her climb up Dunvegan tor and stood gazing out over the valley. Across the waters of the loch, the Mother Mountain still slept, nestled in her earthly blankets. No fires burned there for Bree to see today. Instead, a sigh of contentment drifted to her on the air as, heather rippling in the breeze, the Mother of Dunvegan snuggled deeper into her living bed.

Following that purple wave, Bree's gaze rolled along the foothills and into Dunvegan Village. She could just make out the earthy, single-story post office of the quiet community. She knew Morag MacKenzie would be sitting behind the counter on her break at this hour, enjoying a cuppa and a *McVities* biscuit or two. The *Closed for Tea* sign was too small for her to see from this distance, but she knew it hung from the handle of the unlocked door all the same.

She chuckled. *Maybe I could belong here.* She let her gaze drift across the valley around her, then she continued up the empty hillside.

No sheep today. She smiled. *Just as well.* She was grateful not to have to explain her visit to the Duirnish Stone yet again.

"We've plenty of more sightly places, if it's a good walk you're wanting," Hamish had countered. "I could pack us a lunch. We'd be back in plenty of time to welcome the day's guests."

A picnic with Hamish... Bree considered the fleece-strewn hillside. Despite the steep incline, the view carried her breathless from the Mother Mountain to the waters of the loch and out to the sea. The perfect place for a quiet rest. In her mind's eye, she could almost see a worn, handwoven blanket spread out upon the hill, stones guarding the corners from the gripping wind and Hamish leaning back on his elbow as his brown curls dashed in the breeze. *...Tempting. Very tempting.*

Bree closed her eyes and shivered. *But, not today.*

He had offered to walk up the mountain with her or just drive her there and back, but Bree had refused. "It's something I need to do myself," she insisted. He had looked at her so strangely before relenting. She could still see him—hands on his hips, brow furrowed, brown eyes dark and brooding. She wondered, what did he see that made him yield?

In the end, he had tucked her into her Citroën with a smile. "Caitlin warned me. Ye've an oddness about ye an' do things your own way."

Bree opened her eyes. There, at the top of the hill, she could clearly see the Old Man. The yellow stripes of his kilt shone in the sunlight, radiant against the blue and green of his plaid and the earth. He stood beside the single, three-meter monolith, tall and silent like the stone. Grey hair and beard drifting in the breeze, he leaned against the staff in his left hand.

As his grey eyes met hers, an ache pierced her left shoulder and Bree reached to rub it. The throbbing lessened, but she knew the relief was only temporary. The pain spread from her shoulder blade to the front, as it had in her journey last night. No doubt, it was meant as a reminder.

As if I could forget.

Black hair dancing in the wind, Bree climbed the rest of the way to the top of the hill. Stopping before him, she bowed her head.

"Welcome back, Raven Child."

Bree placed her right hand over her heart. "Peace be between us..."

The Old Man smiled and drew his staff over his heart. "*...now and through all time.*"

Lifting her gaze, she stared into his ancient, grey eyes. No light spilled forth from them to bathe her today. Instead, they considered her coolly, their opalescent light hooded and pooling in their depths.

He knows. He knows why I have come.

The voice of her Bear Ally whispered through her. "*But the question must be spoken for the answer to be received.*"

Bree held the Old Man's gaze. "Who are they, the exiles on the Mother Mountain?"

"*Souls lost in time. They have been dead so long the world they knew has died, too.*"

"What do you mean?"

The Old Man adjusted his staff and lifted his chin. "*You have seen them for yourself, Raven Child. You know, they are not of this era.*"

"No," Bree shook her head. "Their clothes are of a much older make and style. Even their greaves and bracers are fashioned... differently."

He nodded. "*These are the products of an ancient way of life, one not seen upon this earth for millennia. Yet, once it existed, even thrived here upon this land. Do you not remember?*"

Bree frowned. "Remember?"

His grey eyes held her in their steady gaze. "*They were your kith and kin.*"

The wind whipped through Bree's hair, sending it thrashing across her cheeks and forehead. Closing her eyes, she turned her face into the gust. *Related to me? How? When?* She scanned her soul for a memory. As the black strands of her hair shifted to stream behind her, voices too low to understand drifted past her on the wind.

"What happened to them?"

"*They died. Slaughtered by raiders from beyond the world they knew, they died without warning and without the chance to fight according to their custom, by champion. And every last one of the local community perished, including those in the Sacred Enclosure trained to transition souls into rebirth. At first, they hoped someone of their extended tribe— one of their kith and kin still living on another shore—would come to care for them, to open the doorway between This World and the Otherworld and free them to continue the cycle of Becoming. But no one came."* He shrugged. *"Then the world changed. Those of their extended tribe died or were interwoven with others until no one remained alive who could have spoken their names or remembered their ways. Thus they have waited— trapped on the earth sacred to their people and unable to cross without the assistance of one of their kind, again living, Awakened and Initiated."*

Bree turned to face the Mother Mountain. She stood there, gazing across the waters of the loch to the rising contours of the sacred hill. No torchlight twinkled on that horizon. Through the flat, overcast daylight, a pair of brownish-green eyes opened to meet her own.

"You could help them, Raven Child. You could release them."

"How?"

"Honor their ways. Seek within you their ritual for crossing the dead. Open the door for them back to living."

Bree shifted her gaze back to the Old Man. Opalescent light shimmered in the depths of his grey eyes. "They mentioned reasons to help and reasons to refuse. What would be the reasons for me to say no?"

The Old Man nodded. *"Once you agree to assist these exiles, you will be able to remember your lifetimes amongst them. Remembering will etch its mark upon your energy body. Others of their kind will recognize you, even seek you out for assistance. The dead can be... persistent."*

Bree let her gaze drift out across the valley as she considered his words. The wind still tugged at her hair, but the voices she heard earlier were silent. Although she could not see them, she knew the eyes of the community were watching her.

"But, wouldn't it benefit everyone for them to make Transition and return to the Otherworld? My Allies have taught me a soul needs to integrate the teachings and experiences of a given lifetime before choosing a new imperative to carry her into the next lifetime and onward through the journey of Becoming." She looked at the Old Man. "They have taught me, also, when one person is healed, everyone is healed. Is that not correct?"

"It would, and it is." He smiled. *"In this case, especially."*

Bree furrowed her brow. "What does that mean?"

"To find your way back to the living, you must first let go of the dead."

29

Bree sat in her Citroën. From her spot in the pullout, she could still see the Duirnish Stone, standing tall and watchful on the top of the tor. The Old Man was nowhere to be seen. Still, she knew he was watching.

She considered his words. *"Once you agree to assist these exiles, you will be able to remember your lifetimes amongst them. Remembering will etch its mark upon your energy body. Others of their kind will recognize you, even seek you out for assistance."* Would that be so bad? More importantly, would bearing that Gift be in keeping with her promise of Service?

Instinctively, she reached up and ran her fingers along the *clootie* hanging from the rearview mirror. *What would Mother Bríghid say?*

"To tend the Sacred Flame of Life is to cultivate Balance, Flow and Oneness," Bríghid's voice spilled through her. *"And to tend the Sacred Flame, you must be able to see it in all its manifestations—This Worldly and Otherworldly, including manifestations of Soul."*

Bree's eyes found the rearview mirror. Instead of her own reflection, Bríghid's radiant gaze shone back at her. White light flashed from the goddess' eyes and Bree's forehead pulsed.

"Help them, Raven Child. Set them free and restore Balance. Allow the dance of Life to flow again."

"How?"

"Tend the Sacred Flame. Remember their way of opening the doorway between This World and Source. Let the Light of the Sacred Flame guide them Home."

Bree frowned. Dropping her gaze, she gripped the steering wheel with both hands. Above her, the Duirnish Stone stood watching.

Bríghid's voice drew her back. *"Still you hesitate. Why, mo Ghrá... my Love?"*

Bree shifted her gaze to meet Bríghid's. "Tell me, Mother— after all these years of studying and training, of cultivating and awakening in the Celtic Way—after all that, in remembering their way of crossing souls, am I being untrue to our Way? To our lineage? To you?"

Her forehead pulsed, then her vision blurred. She stood before a single flame burning in an ancient, earthen brazier. As she bowed, Bríghid's voice—feminine, ancient, loving—seared through her.

"The Sacred Flame of Life burns at the heart of All. It is the fire out of which all life arises and through which all returns to Source. Many have glimpsed this flame and endeavored to describe it, thus many names exist for it. Just as many pathways lead to it.

"No one path is more perfect, more sacred than another. All are equally blessed. They differ only in the experience of their Walking.

"To remember their way to this flame, the Way of these exiles, is to activate yet another pathway within you. In so doing, you will come to perceive the Sacred Flame of Life through new eyes. This is a Sacred Gift, an Awakening, for it opens the soul to a deeper vision and understanding."

Bree considered the flame before her. "Am I ready for such an Initiation, Mother?"

Bríghid appeared beside her. With a tender smile, the goddess grasped her hand. Gentle warmth enfolded Bree as the goddess cradled her hand upon Her heart. *"Trust, chiya. Let Love show you the Way."*

The flames danced before her. Gazing into them, the world opened for Bree. The faces of loved ones and strangers alike rippled into and out of view. She witnessed the earth in its becoming, even the cosmos spiraling in its endless dance. As one, they called to her—*Love, Love, Love.*

"I choose to trust in Love," Bree whispered.

Bríghid nodded as she lifted Bree's hand from Her heart.

"Love, Love, Love," the voices of life called. Bree swore they grew louder as the goddess stretched her hand closer to the flame. Power prickled across her skin, running from her fingertips up her palm and across the back of her hand. As Bríghid guided her hand ever closer to that fire, power raced through her and her whole being tingled.

Bree's heart pounded. So close now. Her hand slowed just this side of the flame. Her breath quickened. She had never dared come so near it on her own before.

Bríghid's eyes caught her gaze. *"Trust."*

Bree exhaled slowly. "I choose to trust in Love."

With a nod, Bríghid released Bree's hand into the fire.

Power, raw and unbounded, exploded through her, searing her world in white. Her breath rasped hard and ragged, and she struggled for balance in the surge. As the brilliance swallowed her, she gasped and everything went black.

30

Somewhere a bell was ringing. Bree heard it. No, she felt it. A relentless churning, it rocked and reeled her world, twirling her in its bounding dance. Her mind struggled to keep pace and she stumbled. Tossed upon the current, she realized the rhythm was... *familiar.*

Bree's eyes snapped open with a start. Inhaling deeply, she blinked once, twice. The steering wheel arched before her and she grasped it tightly. With an exhale, she lowered her forehead to rest between her hands.

Just breathe.

Fire blazed in her vision. She blinked again, without relief. Reddish-gold, the flames licked and flickered all around her. *Love, Love, Love,* they called to her.

She closed her eyes. *Look past the Otherworldly. Peer through the Sacred Flame and see again This World.* Bree took a deep, slow breath, then opened her eyes. Flames leapt and swirled before her. Narrowing her gaze, she stared into the heart of the fire and called to This World.

The square toes of her boots flickered in the blaze. Locking onto the image, she concentrated on bringing that one, simple object into focus. *Look for the details. Use them like a rope to pull yourself to safety. See the stitching...* How many times had she admired the simple, even strokes that held boot and sole together? Bree often wondered what kind of needle could penetrate such tough hide. *There...* She could just make out the small, even loops of dark thread running along the inseam. As the scuff on the left toe rose into view, the flames receded and she exhaled.

Thump!

Bree sat back hard against the seat. Black eyes met hers. Midnight-black feathers gleamed before her as she stared at an enormous raven, now perched on the hood of the Citroën. Shadowing it from the distance, she could see the curving edges of the Duirnish Stone.

The tor... the pullout... How long have I been here?

The bouncing notes of an Irish jig spilled through the car. As the raven nudged its beak at her, Bree rubbed her eyes and drew a deep breath to orient herself. Returning her gaze to the visitor, she saw two more ravens, wings outstretched, swooping over the front of the Citroën.

"Answer the telephone!"

The female voice rang clearly through her. Staring into the raven's black eyes, Bree frowned. *Telephone? What telephone?*

The song reeled again, echoing through the cabin of the car. Bree blinked and looked around her. A light flashed from the seat next to her, drawing her attention. Her purse rested there, half-open, with some of its contents spilled into view.

"Oh, *my* telephone!"

Blue eyes sparkled before her on the screen. As the jig started anew, Bree slid the telephone the rest of the way out of her bag and gazed at the image of a woman with beautiful, silver hair hanging in a thick plait down her shoulder. *Why would she be calling?* Puzzled, Bree pressed answer.

"Bree? Bree, are you there?"

Still staring at the photo of her cousin, Bree furrowed her brow as she raised the telephone to her ear. "Sibeal?"

"Bríghid be praised!" Relief flooded through the telephone and poured over Bree. "I have been calling and calling! Are you okay? Are you safe?"

Good question... Bree looked around her. She could clearly see her arms, legs and torso, all intact and where they should be. For good measure, she flexed her fingers and shifted her feet on the floor, wiggling her toes. *So far so good.*

Convinced she was physically okay, she gazed further. She sat in the driver's seat of the Citroën. The windows and doors were closed and undamaged, and the interior appeared as cozy and peaceful as she remembered. The hood stretched out in front of her, albeit with the unusual addition of the raven perched on its edge. A glimpse outside confirmed the car stood alone in the pullout. On the tor above her, the Duirnish Stone still stood watching, as twilight darkened the sky. She leaned forward and frowned. *How did it get to be so late?*

"Bree?"

"Sorry..." Bree sat back as she watched the other two ravens circling above the hood of the car. "I was just checking, making sure. And, yes, I am okay and safe." *If a little confused.*

Sibeal sighed. "I sensed your distress, even spilled my tea from the backlash. But when I looked into the Otherworld, I couldn't find you. All I saw was fire. What happened?"

Another good question. "An Initiation." Bree paused, considering her experience. "I guess you could say Mother Bríghid baptized me in the Fire of Creation." When Sibeal remained silent, Bree continued. "I think... It must have overwhelmed me. I seem to have blacked out."

The raven on the hood of her car fluttered its wings, then hopped closer to the windshield. As it tapped its beak gently against the glass, the second raven swooped down and landed behind it. Then the third circled once more overhead before alighting on the hood with its companions. Together, the three birds gazed at Bree.

She stared, her mouth gaping slightly. *Three Ravens. Three Crones. The Council of Three.* The thought came unbidden as the image of three ancient warriors—women dressed in full battle leathers, greaves and bracers—shimmered in her inner eye. She knew these women, at least as they appeared in this lifetime. They were her cousins, Ailene, Cara and Sibeal. They represented the three eldest, third-born daughters of the warrior lineage of Bree's Irish family, and their sole purpose was to support and protect the current *Bean feasa,* namely Bree.

But, they are in Seattle.

The tapping on the windshield grew louder as the first raven pecked harder. Bree reached up and touched the glass with her free hand. The raven dropped its head and rubbed her hand from the other side.

Bree's breath caught in her throat. "Sibeal," she whispered into the telephone, "How? How did you know?"

"I told you, I sensed your distress. I was just sitting down to morning tea, and, all of a sudden, I couldn't breathe. The room started to sway around me and I fell into my seat. Knocked my cup over and spilled my tea across the table. When I looked at the pooling liquid, I saw your face surrounded in flames and realized you were in trouble." Sibeal paused, inhaling. "As soon as I was able, I summoned the Council. We agreed to send the ravens to find and guard you until contact could be re-established."

The raven lifted its head and stared into Bree's eyes. The image of her cousin Cara shimmered into view, then disappeared.

Bree cleared her throat. "You mean, you always know when I am in danger?"

"Danger or distress, yes." Sibeal paused. "In those moments, Raven summons us and allows us to see through Her eyes to assist you. It is part of how we support and protect you."

The other two ravens on the hood of her car hopped forward, taking up positions on either side of their companion.

"Bree," Sibeal's voice enfolded her. "Ailene spoke the truth when we met three months ago. You are no longer alone."

31

Light flooded the cabin of the Citroën as the sound of gravel churning in the pullout filled Bree's awareness. She lifted her gaze to the rearview mirror and instantly regretted it. Two headlights seared her vision from directly behind the car. She closed her eyes and rubbed them with her free hand.

"Grrrack!" The ravens on the hood of the car shrieked in complaint.

"Bree, what's happening?" Sibeal's voice cut through her. "A light just flashed, blinding me."

Bree massaged the inner corners of her eyes. *Me, too.* She drew breath to explain, then hesitated. Footsteps rattled the gravel of the pullout, and an image of Hamish standing beside his open, driver's-side door flashed in her inner vision.

"Bree?" Hamish called from behind her car. "Bree? Can ye hear me?"

Raindrops pattered on the roof of the Citroën. *Love, Love, Love,* they sang to her. She knew that song. She had first heard it three months ago, during her visit to Seattle. And she could hear it now, blessing the earth and all of living life with each splatter, each splotch. The tears of the Goddess. The joy of the Goddess—Bree now realized—Her unbridled Love for creation, pouring out in

123

sacred offering, blessing the earth in its timeless song. *Love, Love, Love.*

"Bree!"

Sibeal's voice echoed through the Citroën as the front raven croaked loudly. Bree opened her eyes and touched the windshield where the raven stood, its beak pressed against the glass. Once again the raven rubbed its head, tracing the outline of her hand.

"I'm okay, Sibeal. A friend just pulled up behind me and I looked into his headlights."

"Well," her cousin sighed. "At least we know the link works."

"Bree!" Hamish appeared at her window. Resting his hands upon the glass, he leaned toward the door. Concern etched his face as he peered through the streaking rain into the Citroën.

Releasing the windshield, Bree waived her free hand, then gestured to her telephone.

Water spilled down his curls as he mouthed, "Are ye all right?"

Bree offered him a wan smile before nodding once. She saw his broad shoulders heave with a sigh. As the rain soaked his dark hair, he rested his forehead against the glass. But his eyes never left her face.

"Sibeal, I have to go."

"Are you sure? Maybe I should talk you home?"

Genuine care flooded to her through the telephone, from the ravens perched on the hood of the car and from Hamish, while all around her the rain sang its ageless refrain—*Love, Love, Love.* A tear slid down Bree's cheek. *Is this how belonging feels?*

"No. You and Raven have done your jobs." Bree stared into Hamish's deep, brown eyes. Rain streaked his cheeks as he stood watching her. Instinctively, Bree reached up and pressed her free hand to the window. "Besides, Hamish is here. He will see me safely back to Heather House."

Sibeal hesitated before sighing deeply. "Well, since someone is there with you, I will let you go. But remember, we're here for you if you need us."

Another tear slid down Bree's cheek. She swallowed to clear the lump aching in her throat. "I will. Thank you, cousin. And please, tell Cara and Ailene I am truly grateful."

"Crrruck!"

As the call disconnected, the three ravens perched on the hood of the Citroën croaked in unison. Then in a flutter of feathers they lifted, one by one, off the car. The last to depart, the raven closest to the windshield hovered before her. Black eyes locked with hers and, for a moment, her cousin's bright blue eyes flashed into view. Then the raven was gone. Only the rain remained, pattering its endless refrain—*Love, Love, Love.*

Her car door opened and Bree snapped her head to the right to see a soaking wet Hamish standing beside her. Folding his arms across the top of the car, he leaned in, his body shielding her from the rain. His eyes scanned her from head to toe and back again before he heaved another sigh.

"Well, ye appear none the worse for wear. Are ye injured? Do ye have need of any care?"

Bree shook her head, blinking back tears. She had not expected such genuine concern, from her cousins or the man before her. "No... no, I'm fine. Really."

Hamish grunted. "Can ye drive? Or shall I carry ye?"

"I can drive." She hesitated. "I think."

Hamish stared a while before nodding his head. "Then I'll follow. To see ye safely home."

He stood there looking at her, his dark eyes shimmering in the rain. As he closed the car door, Bree reached out and held it open.

"Thanks, Hamish... for coming... for caring enough to come find me."

A fire crackled to life in the hearth of Heather House. Brushing off his hands, Hamish stood up and replaced the wrought iron fireplace screen before turning to face Bree. She sat on the sofa, shivering visibly despite the throw blankets wrapped around her shoulders. Pulling the white Heather House bathrobe more tightly around himself, Hamish stepped toward her and rubbed her back and arms.

"There's the fire lit. That should help tae warm ye."

Bree nodded as she snuggled more deeply into the blankets. She had started shivering on the way back to Heather House. Forcing herself to focus only on This World while driving, she was able to ignore it at first. Now, she realized the endless shaking was somehow significant. If only she could remember why.

Hamish sat down on the arm of the sofa opposite her. His eyes scanned her from head to toe and back again, concern slowly etching his face. Bree knew the shivering was worrying him. She fought to control it, but only made it worse. With a frown, Hamish stood, walked to the corner cabinet and opened the glass door.

Bree let her gaze drift back toward the fireplace. A bowl of apples rested on the table in front of her. Without thinking, she reached forward and grabbed an apple from the pile. Her mouth was watering as she lifted it and took a bite. She chewed slowly and sweet juice spilled down her throat. Swallowing the fragrant flesh, she could not remember the last time anything tasted so good.

A highball glass appeared before her, hovering directly in front of her face. A dark liquid pooled in its bottom half. Bree leaned back to see Hamish standing next to her, the glass dangling from his fingertips. She took another bite of apple.

"T'll warm ye."

Bree shifted her gaze to meet his and swallowed. "What is it?"

"Single malt. Twelve year, Highland Park."

Bree raised her eyebrows and reached for the glass. "Excellent choice."

As Hamish settled back onto the arm of the other sofa, Bree washed another bite of her apple down with a sip of whiskey. With each swallow, warmth coursed slowly through her and her body stopped shaking. *Energy depletion*, she noted mentally. Her interactions with the Old Man and Bríghid that afternoon had exhausted her energetic supplies. While the apple and whiskey were a start toward recovery, she needed food and soon.

She grabbed a napkin from the table, wrapped the apple core in it and placed it on her lap. When she looked up, Hamish was watching her. He leaned closer, his dark eyes searching her face.

"Better?"

Bree offered him a thin smile. "Getting there. Thanks."

"Ye had me worried." He leaned back, his eyes resting on her face. "When ye were nae here for afternoon check in..." His expression tensed. "Ach, I envisioned the worst and went tae find ye as soon as I could."

"I'm so sorry." She brushed a strand of hair out of her eyes. "How did you know where to find me?"

"Jock." He shook his head. "I did nae know where ye'd gone nor where to start looking for ye. So, I made a few calls. Morag, Maggie, but nothing. Then Jock mentioned he'd seen ye atop the tor." He sighed. "So I rushed over, praying tae find ye there."

Bree reached out and touched his knee with her hand. Her fingers tingled from the warmth of his skin. She knew she should explain, tell him what had happened to delay her. As he folded her hand into his own, she wondered, *Would he understand?* She searched his eyes with her own. She just did not know.

"Thank you," she whispered instead.

He nodded and they sat a while in silence. When her stomach growled, he chuckled.

"Are ye hungry?"

Bree laughed. "Famished, actually."

He stood up and took her empty glass and the napkin containing her apple core. "Well, ye rest here a while. I'll see if my clothes are dry and get ye something from the kitchen. Nothing grand, mind. But enough to satisfy."

Bree watched him walk toward the kitchen. "Hamish," she called before he reached the door. As he turned back to face her, she smiled. "How many guests arrived while I was away?"

"Five." He nodded. "I got them settled well enough. And their breakfast orders are on the counter in the kitchen." Then he turned and walked out of the room.

Bree sighed. "Good man."

33

Bree sat on the floor of her room in Heather House. A single candle cast its light at the center of the circle she had set moments earlier. Legs folded under her, hands resting on her knees, she stared into the gentle glow. Just beyond her Ordinary vision, golden-red flames blazed in the Otherworld.

The Sacred Flame.

So, it was still with her. She had lost sight of it during her conversation with Sibeal and the visit from the ravens. Still a bit disoriented, she forced herself to focus solely on This World as she ate the sandwich Hamish made for her and prepped the kitchen for tomorrow's breakfasts. She had all but forgotten about that fire, until she set the candle down on her bedroom floor.

She lifted her hands, extending her palms toward the flame. Power prickled across her skin, running from her fingertips, up her palms and into her arms and shoulders. Deepening her breath, she exhaled slowly.

"Breathe into the power," the voice of her Bear Ally whispered through her awareness. *"It is a Sacred Gift. Drink it in, chiya. Let it flow through you. Let it replenish and restore you."*

"How?"

"Trust in Love." Warmth spread through Bree's chest as two

paws reached from the Otherworld to rest upon her. *"And remember, we are with you."*

Bree closed her eyes as Bear's loving presence seeped into her. Wrapping herself in that tender comfort, she drew a slow, steadying breath and slipped across the Veil.

All around her fire blazes. Golden-red, the flames flicker and lash, reaching to draw her into their dance. As one, they call to her—Love, Love, Love. Extending her hands before her, palms upward, Bree bows her head in honoring.

"Blessed is the Mystery."

The flames lick at her hands, then disappear into her fingers and palms. She waits for her limbs to catch and dance with the blaze. Instead, white light infuses them and spills up the sides of her arms to her shoulders. Where it shimmers, her skin prickles.

Brighid's voice—feminine, ancient, loving—whispers from the flames. "Gently, now. Take it in a little more slowly this time."

Bree nods. Her gaze fixed on the light permeating her hands, she inhales a slow, deep breath. The light blanches and seeps into her, flooding up her arms and turning them white.

"This time," Brighid whispers, "drink from your toes."

Bree drops her gaze to her feet. Golden-red flames lap between her toes. She wriggles them and stares. The sides gleam white.

"Gently, now."

Inhaling, Bree watches the light pour into her feet and spill up her shins. Another breath and the light floods her hips, pooling to fill her pelvis. With her next inhale, the light rushes through her stomach as the light from her shoulders pours into her chest. She feels her throat filling and struggles to catch her breath. Panic shudders through her.

"We are with you."

Bear presses her paws against Bree's chest. The gesture should offer comfort, but it drives the light deeper into Bree's throat. She shivers as terror engulfs her.

"The flame is Love. Pure, unconditional Love." The voice of her mother, Bríde, rises from the fire and wraps around Bree. Before her, the

image of Bride flickers to life in the golden-red flames and smiles. "Just like you."

Bree thrashes in her struggle. Unable to speak, her eyes grip those of her mother. Help, she pleads mentally.

Bride steps closer. "Remember Love. Remember those who love you."

Unable to focus on anything but the light spilling into her neck, Bree shakes her head.

"Emily and Rose. They love you."

An image of Emily, Bree's aunt and foster mother, shimmers into view in the fire before Bree. Emily smiles, then gestures to her left. Her daughter, Rose appears in the fire. "You can do this, cousin."

"And Gwen, she loves you."

Gwen appears in the fire. She reaches out to Bree, then draws back her arms. She nods. "Trust in Love."

"Your kinswoman, Caitlin. Your cousins Heather, Connor and Declan. And so many others, chiya. So many, like me and, of course, Brighid."

"Drink it in, my Love." Brighid's voice echoes through the fire. "Trust."

Three ravens ripple into view as they fly through the fire. Blue eyes hover in Bree's awareness, then they are gone.

Bree's eyes search out her mother. Her whole being trembles as she struggles to prevent the light from rushing into her head.

Sorrow seeps from her mother's eyes. She steps closer to Bree. "The flame is Love. Pure, unconditional Love. Just like you. Just like your soul. Remember the flame of your soul. Trust in Love and let the two become one."

Bear's paws press against her chest. "Trust in the flame of your soul."

White light bursts from Bree's head as the brilliance swallows her. Power races through her, searing the threads and fibers of her consciousness. Her breath comes hard and fast as she struggles in the surge.

Brighid's voice whispers. "Do you remember, my Love? That night in the grove with your niece? The night you welcomed Fiona to the family tradition."

White light roils around Bree, spilling faces that coalesce and rise out of the flames. Before her, an image of her niece Fiona sits holding a candle in a glass globe as Bríghid considers the young girl.

"Everything is sacred," Bríghid explains to the young novice as Bree watches. "And every flame is sacred. Both this flame..." Bríghid gestures toward the candle flame before placing her hand over Fiona's heart. "...and this flame. Tend them both with equal care."

As the images dissolve back into the churning flames, only Bríghid remains. Standing before her, the goddess holds Bree's gaze.

"Now, mo Ghrá... my Love." Bríghid prompts. "Kindle your own fire and claim your light."

"Remember the flame of your soul," Bree repeats her mother's words. They crackle and hiss through the whiteness around her. Why, Bree wonders. What is her mother trying to show her? Why would her mother direct her to the flame of the soul? "Because," she whispers, understanding prickling along her limbs, "fire cannot consume fire."

How old had she been when she first experienced the soul as a sacred flame? Eight? Nine? Fiona's age, she marvels. It had taken her years to attempt to move through the Otherworld in that form. Existing as pure flame seems so strange to her, even after all these years. And the very idea makes her shiver.

But here, now, pure flame is what she needs most to be.

Inhaling deeply, Bree stares into the whiteness engulfing her. Consciously slowing her breath, she calls to the flame at the center of her being. White fire roils, threatening to pull her into it, to drown her in its searing tide. Her breath quickens as panic rushes through her. Fighting for calm, she closes her eyes and calls again to the flame of her soul.

A blue flame flickers in the depths. Awareness slowly dissolving, Bree turns her consciousness toward it, then hesitates. "What if I lose myself there, too?"

"Trust." Bear's presence steadies her. "Trust in the flame of your soul."

Struggling to keep the blue flame in focus, Bree whispers, "I choose to trust in Love." Then, with an exhale, she lets go of everything around her and dives into the flame of her soul.

34

Blue fire blazes. Where Bree's arms, legs and body should be, light streams outward, then swirls back in upon itself. Her consciousness flows with the timeless dance. She knows no heat, no discomfort. Instead, a deep sense of peace permeates her. Watching the endless cascade, she marvels. "It's like being inside a sapphire."

She tries to close her eyes, then remembers—she has no eyes to close. Here she is pure light. No body, no form, only endless, flowing flame. Sinking into the flow, she lets her consciousness drift.

"Mo Ghrá... my Love..." Bríghid's voice ripples the periphery of Bree's awareness.

"Hmmmmm?"

"Come, my Love." Bríghid's words sparkle like fireworks in the flow.

Bree hesitates, unwilling to relinquish the comfort of this place. "Come? Where?"

"Remember what brought you here. Claim your light and stand within the Sacred Flame."

Golden-red fire flickers all around her. Bree can see it now, just beyond her soul flame. "What do I do?"

"Drink it in. Let it become part of you. Let the two flames dance as one."

Bree considers the golden-red sea stretching around her. A frisson of fear shivers through her, dulling the blue of her flame.

"Fire cannot consume fire." Bear reminds her.

Bree would smile if she had a mouth and lips. Instead she replies, "And the flame is Love. Pure, unconditional Love. Just like me." Letting her consciousness flow to the very edges of her soul flame, she adds, "And I choose to trust in Love." Then she sinks into the Sacred Flame.

Golden-red fire seeps into her. Flowing from all directions, it rushes to fill her. Bree watches the red and blue flames swirl inward together as power pulses and builds within her. Where the two flames rub, heat prickles and snaps. As the intensity builds, Bree's flame begins to shake.

"Now," Bríghid whispers, "claim your light."

Silver light flashes, like lightning splitting the sky of Bree's soul. Heat blazing, white flames flare outward from the center of her to the edges of her soul flame. As her world sears white once more, Bree affirms, "I choose to trust in Love."

Another flash, and Bree finds herself standing at the center of her soul flame. Blue fire streams outward, then swirls back in upon itself. All around her, the Sacred Flame flickers. Where its golden-red light flows into the blue of her soul flame, white etches her. She smiles, as a deep sense of peace permeates her.

"Welcome home, Bree Nic Bhríde, mo Ghrá... my Love."

Bree shifts her gaze as Bríghid emerges out of the fire. "Thank you, Mother." She bows her head in loving gratitude. As she rises, she frowns. "Is this their way Home, too? The community of exiles?"

Bríghid shakes her head. "No, my Love."

Bree sighs with relief. Still in awe of her own transition, she could not imagine guiding each one of the exiles through this process. "Then how? How do I guide them Home?"

Bríghid gestures behind her. An enormous wooden door appears within the Sacred Flame. Without thinking, Bree steps closer to the door. Bríghid's hand on her shoulder stops her.

"This is their doorway Home."

35

Bree stood in the den of Heather House, her telephone in one hand and a steaming mug of tea in the other. Gazing out the large bay window across the loch to the Mother Mountain, she watched the heather ripple and sway in the wind. As the purple blurred and streaked her vision, the wooden door from her journey the night before rose clearly into view. Although no eyes stared back at her, she knew the community of exiles was watching.

I'm coming, she whispered mentally as she took a sip of tea.

"I've confirmed my return flights. I'll be back in ten days." Caitlin's lilting voice drew Bree back to their telephone conversation and prickled along Bree's skin.

Bree paused and considered the stinging. "If you want to stay longer, Hamish and I have things well in hand here. Must be good to be home."

Caitlin chuffed and Bree's skin burned. "Home?" The word rattled Bree's bones and she had to shift her stance to prevent spilling her tea. "Aye, I suppose," her kinswoman continued. "But, truth be told, I am missing Skye."

Bree swallowed another sip of tea as a hawk skimmed the waters of the loch. She had come to love this view in the two months she had been caretaking Heather House. She could understand her friend's desire to see it again. Her skin prickled once more and Bree shivered. Was there something more?

"Has it changed much?"

"Cape Breton?" Caitlìn chuckled. "Ach, no. Life here is the same as it always was. The pipes still sing the day to sleep and the sun to wake. The sea still fills the fishermen's nets, and the hills still whisper of yesterday."

Bree could taste the salty air, heavy on her lips, and hear the song of the bagpipes rumbling with the surf. An ache throbbed along her bones and she wondered if it were her own.

"Cape Breton is lovely as ever. But, it seems, I have changed." Caitlìn sighed. "Mother warned me. Well, she tried to, at least."

The voice of Caitlìn's mother whispered through Bree. "Go now, if ye can, before the song of Skye thrums in your veins. For the Isle will claim ye and ye'll never want to leave. Skye never lets go of Her own."

The sun broke through the darkening clouds and glinted off the waters of the loch. Bree closed her eyes, shielding them from the sudden brilliance. For a heartbeat, through the shimmering light, she could clearly see raven-black hair above a green woolen cloak.

"Tha bròn orm... I'm sorry..." A man's voice droned.

The man from the community of exiles. Who is he? Snapshot images cascaded through her inner vision—spiraling lines that stretched and interlocked endlessly, three women tending a fire, the sea rolling out to the horizon. Snippets of dreams lost or forgotten, Bree was not sure which. And what they had to do with the man in the green woolen cloak, she did not know. Or, she could not remember. Pressing her eyes more tightly closed, she strained to summon a face, but the image was gone.

Caitlìn's voice broke her concentration. "I'm off to Peterborough tomorrow. Then I'll catch the train to Toronto and fly home."

Home. The word reverberated through Bree, leaving in its path a deep ache of longing.

Bree opened her eyes. The waters of the loch flowed peacefully on the other side of the bay window. "Send me your itinerary and we'll be sure to meet you."

"Will do."

As the call disconnected, Bree slid her telephone into her back pocket. Sipping her still-warm tea, she let her gaze drift. Across the loch, the Mother Mountain stood as She had for eons, keeping gentle watch over Her children. Swallowing another sip, Bree wondered, how many had left these lands only to ache to see it again?

"They never come home."

Bree's head snapped to her left, toward the woman's voice. So familiar, she could almost envision the face that should be there. But the space beside her was empty. Looking around the den, Bree turned in a slow circle. Only the sofas and pillows stared back at her. Even the face, she realized with a frown, was lost beyond recall.

Returning her gaze to the Mother Mountain, Bree lifted her mug only to find it empty. She sighed. What was it Caitlin's mother had said? *"Skye never lets go of Her own."*

"Well, rest easy Lady," Bree spoke aloud to the Isle. "Another of your daughters is coming home soon."

36

Rain lashed the outer walls of Heather House and streaked down the big bay window. As the glass rattled with the wind, Bree shivered and settled deeper into the sofa. What had Hamish called it? "A night no fit for man nay beast." He had called to check on her when the rain started to pummel the house. "Best ye keep a candle close. The power might go out. It oft does when the *Bean-Sidhe* howls."

The lights flickered for a second time and Bree waited, her eyes on the lamp beside her. With a fire in the hearth and a cluster of candles on the table, she was prepared for a dark night. But the lights continued to shine. *So far, at least.*

As the wind clawed at the windows, Bree pulled the throw blanket off the back of the sofa and drew it around her shoulders. Drawing the cover up to her neck, she gazed into the glowing fireplace. Tonight especially, she was grateful for its warmth.

Those poor people. She was expecting a couple from Dublin, the only guests she had booked for the night. They were returning from a stay on the Isle of Lewis, across the Minch. "The seas are too rough," the woman had screamed into the telephone, fighting to be louder than the howling wind. "The ferry cannot make the crossing."

Just as well, Bree gazed into the fire. *I have other concerns this night.*

The community of exiles. With the house empty, tonight would be her best opportunity to cross them.

The window groaned as the rain continued its lashing. Bree checked the time on her telephone. Eight o'clock. She doubted any guests would be dropping in at this point. No doubt most people had already sought shelter from the storm. Still, in the past weeks filling in for Caitlìn, Bree had learned one thing for certain—the doors of a B&B were always open.

I'll wait one more hour. Then I'll lock the door.

Bree set her telephone down on the table and snuggled back into the sofa. As she leaned back, lightning flashed, illuminating the room in freeze-frame stillness. Thunder rattled the windows and shook the house. Around her the lights flickered once, twice, then dimmed to darkness. Bree realized she was holding her breath and forced herself to exhale.

The fire still burned in the fireplace. Bree leaned forward and looked around her. Shadows stretched and danced on the walls of the den. For a moment, gazing toward the front window, Bree thought she could see eyes glittering in the dark of the fire-lit room.

"They were your kith and kin." The voice of the Old Man echoed through the room.

Bree leaned back against the sofa cushions. She could remember other past lives of her soul. The idea was definitely not new to her. She was even certain the two kilted men she had glimpsed on her drive to Skye were parts of her soul from previous lifetimes on the Isle. But, a life amongst the community of exiles? That she could not recall. *Not yet, anyway.* Gazing into the fire, she sighed. Why did the idea of being one of them fill her with such sorrow?

The flames flickered in the fireplace. Letting her gaze soften, Bree drifted.

A gentle humming spilled through the room. Bree sensed fingers moving, guiding threads into a pattern, into a weaving. As the unseen woman shaped the tapestry, Bree swayed with the woman's wordless song. Floating on the melody, Bree slipped into the Otherworld.

Feet bare upon the earth, Bree walks in a moonlit forest, autumn leaves crunching with each step. The strap of her bag pulls heavy across her shoulders and she stops to shift it. Stretching her back, she gazes up at the sky. So many stars. Could he see them, too? Were the stars the same on the Sacred Isle? Or did he gaze into the eyes of the Goddess herself from there?

Cold shivers through her and she pulls her woolen wrap more tightly around her. Rounding the bend, the sea stretches dark and brooding before her. She pauses, as she has for so many moons, and casts her gaze upon the waters.

"Come back to me," she calls.

"They never come home."

Bree's head snaps toward the woman's voice. Instead of a face, she stares into the golden-red fire of the Sacred Flame. The wooden door from her journey stands before her. As the door slowly opens, she hesitates and looks behind her. She is alone.

"Good-bye, my love," she whispers, then steps into the open doorway.

Lightning flashed. Bree jumped in her seat on the sofa, then shivered. All around her, eyes shimmered in the darkness of Heather House.

With a sigh, she stood and headed to lock the front door.

"Okay," she whispered. "I'm coming."

37

Golden-red fire blazes. Bree stands alone, staring at the wooden door rising out of the flames. To her left, the fire shudders and Brighid emerges out of the blaze. As Bree bows to the goddess, her Raven Ally spirals out of the flames and perches upon Brighid's outstretched arm.

"You have decided?"

Bree nods to the Mother of her lineage. "I choose to restore Balance. I choose to set the community of exiles free, to guide them Home."

Raven tilts her head. "You do this from a sense of duty?"

Bree gazes at the wooden door. Is that it? Duty? A sense of obligation? Is that what brought her to this moment? The years of training, the endless questioning, and the often harrowing initiations, were they nothing more than personal responsibility? Bree stares at the door shimmering with the flames. Maybe in the beginning, she realizes, but not anymore. No. She has seen and experienced enough to know— the Otherworld is real. And, more importantly, she cares what happens.

"I offer to do this," Bree faces her Allies, "because it is the right thing to do. I choose to restore Balance as an act of Love."

"Then we are with you." Brighid bows her head to Bree. As the goddess straightens, she lifts her arm and launches Raven into flight.

"Crrruck!"

Bree lifts her gaze skyward. As her eyes meet those of Raven, her awareness locks with that of her Ally and she is flying. Wings stretching midnight-black against the currents, she glides through the Otherworld. Feathers quiver on the wind and colors wash over and through her, blurring the boundaries. Then her arms stretch taut against the currents and her body leans, pressing in a spiral downward, downward, downward.

Bree stands in darkness. Her feet bare upon the earth, she turns slowly sunwise. Spreading her hands wide at her sides, she opens her palms to the earth to affirm her peaceful intent.

Small pinpoints of light spark to life and hover in mid-air. As they slowly drift to close a circle around her, Bree continues to turn sunwise. Everywhere she looks, she can see them now, eyes glittering in the dark. Turning more slowly, her own eyes trace subtle outlines. Women and men stand all around her. Their faces and clothing obscured in the shadows, their eyes are firmly focused on her.

Bree takes another step to the right and stops. Fierce, green eyes lock upon her own. Bree's breath catches in her throat and her body tenses. She prepares to step away from the woman now standing before her, but her body refuses. Shifting her gaze, she exhales. Blue ink spirals down the left side of the woman's face and shimmers in the darkness.

"Sìochan duit... Peace be upon Ye." Britomaris bows her head in welcome.

"And upon you." Bree bows in return.

Eyes glitter around the circle. Britomaris' voice is a whisper. "Have Ye decided?"

"I have."

The darkness presses closer. Shivering slightly, Bree glances over her shoulder. From the corners of her eyes she can almost see the people gathering closer to her. Woven cloaks and leather greaves waver in the shadows, then disappear.

Bree smiles. "Gather your people. It is time to go Home."

38

"Ye will help us? Set us free?" Britomaris stares at Bree, green eyes shimmering in the darkness.

Bree nods. "I can guide you to the doorway Home, but the rest is up to you. Are you and your people ready?"

The woman's gaze flows around the glittering circle. As her eyes alight on each individual, one by one each pair of eyes blinks in confirmation. Completing the circuit, Britomaris' eyes meet those of Bree. "Aye, that we are."

Bree inhales a slow, deep breath. Closing her eyes, she whispers mentally. "Mother Brighid, Raven, show me the way."

Hands press her shoulders downward, and Bree bends her knees. As her hands touch the earth, golden-red light pours through her arms and a fire blazes to life. Withdrawing her hands, Bree smiles. Before her, a single flame burns in an ancient earthen brazier.

Gasps echo around her and Bree opens her eyes. The wooden door stands before her, rising out of the golden-red flames.

Bree bows her head. "Blessed is the Mystery."

Voices murmur around the circle, "Blessed is the Mother."

Bree lifts her head to find Britomaris standing before her, torch in hand. Turning to face the woman, Bree gestures toward the Sacred

Flame. "The doorway is now open. Step into the fire and let the Mother welcome you Home."

As Raven settles upon Bree's shoulder, Britomaris steps closer to the fire. Lifting her torch higher, she leans in toward the doorway but remains just outside the flames. Then, with a nod, Britomaris steps away from the fire and points into the darkness.

A torch blazes to life at the indicated spot and hovers in mid-air before moving toward the fire. Beneath the flickering torch, a shape shivers within the darkness. As it draws closer, the torchlight paints the edges, revealing a woman for Bree to see. A long, woven skirt spills toward the earth, swaying above bare feet. Closer now, endless, interlocking spirals emerge out of the darkness, weaving their way across toes and arches. Bree's eyes track the folding shadows upward. Directly before her, a new face blazes in the torchlight. Silver-grey hair falls in plaits around a woman's face etched in countless spirals. The woman's dark eyes find Bree's, then they are gone.

The torch reaches the edge of the fire and pauses. Flickering with the light of both fire and Flame, the woman raises her torch high and peers into the flames.

"She is their Elder," Raven whispers in Bree's ear, "the Keeper of their Way."

The Elder looks back at Britomaris and smiles. Then the Elder's dark eyes again find Bree's and she nods. Turning back to the blaze, the Elder places her torch into the fire and steps into the flames. As she walks toward the door, it opens. Without hesitation, the Elder crosses through the doorway and disappears into the light.

An eerie silence trembles through the encircling shadows and Bree shivers.

"They are waiting, wondering, hoping," Raven whispers.

Bree wants to ask, For what? But the words will not form on her lips. She cannot disturb the aching silence.

A soft mewling cries into the darkness as a blue flame quivers to life, then bursts through the Sacred Flame. Erupting upward, it showers the sky with silvery-blue sparks and is gone.

Hands resting over her heart, Britomaris bows her head beside Bree. "Sin è." Lifting her head, Britomaris lets her arms fall to her sides and casts her gaze into the darkness. With a nod, she points and summons the next exile to the crossing.

In the distance, another torch blazes to life and hovers in mid-air before moving toward the fire. In awe, Bree stares as shapes shiver within the darkness. Flickering in the torchlight, bare feet step silently out of the shadows. Closer now, folds of woven cloth sway red, green and yellow before Bree's gaze. Silver-grey hair spills down a man's back while interlocking circles stretch across his brow. As he steps directly in front of Bree, the man tilts his head, nods and disappears from view.

Another Elder? Bree wonders.

"Correct." Raven answers her unspoken question. "The Mother and the Father united in the Mystery."

The torch reaches the edge of the fire and rises high. Silhouetted in the flickering light, the Elder places his torch into the fire and steps into the flames. Without looking back, the Elder crosses through the open doorway and disappears into the light.

The shadows draw closer. Bree holds her breath as she shivers.

A soft mewling cries into the darkness as a blue flame quivers to life, then bursts through the Sacred Flame. Bree lifts her chin to watch it streak upward and shower the sky with silvery-blue sparks. As the last of the glimmers fade to darkness, Bree exhales with a smile.

"Sin è." Hands resting over her heart, Britomaris bows her head beside Bree before casting her gaze back into the darkness.

One by one, Britomaris summons her people to the crossing. Again and again, Bree watches a single torch approach the fire and become one with the Sacred Flame, releasing a soul to disappear through the open door. Welcome Home, she longs to whisper.

With a soft chirrup, Raven spreads her wings and launches into flight. Bree's gaze follows her Ally until, once more, a torch blazes to life and hovers in mid-air before moving toward the fire.

Beside her, Britomaris turns to face Bree. "Can Ye remember, Child of the Sìdhe?"

Flickering in the torchlight, bare feet step silently out of the shadows. Breath frozen in her throat, Bree knows those feet are stained blue, a remnant of the ritual that called him away from their bonfire, from their shore and to the Sacred Enclosure.

"Can Ye remember, Child of the Sìdhe, the heart Ye knew as well as your own?"

The torch draws closer and Bree shivers. Deep inside her, a soft humming pools and swells. Her breath rasps short and shallow. As the song floods upward, she sees him. Raven-black hair falls unbound above a green woolen cloak.

The humming cascades through her and her vision blurs. Her body sways with the rhythm and the pattern of her working as she weaves threads into a tapestry. Her hands guide themselves with the certainty of experience as her eyes linger upon the rolling waves of the sea.

"Come back to me," she whispers.

Then he is there before her, pack heavy on his shoulder, his cloak slowly slipping down his side. She draws the green wool more tightly around him then, blinking back tears, follows her hands as they trace the spirals she embroidered to mark his acceptance into the Mystery. With a sigh, she lifts her chin and kisses him. Without a word, she watches him board the boat and disappear across the sea.

"Phaisos, my love. Is it truly you?" Bree stares at her past love. "You never returned." She shakes her head. "You left me waiting and you never returned."

Phaisos steps toward her, torch held high. "My training was finally complete. The Sacred Running saw me fully initiated. I would have been free to return to Ye under the next moon." He drops his gaze to the ground. "But that moon rose without me."

Light flashes and Bree gasps as her vision blurs. Phaisos, painted blue, rises slowly to his feet. Staring into the west, his eyes squint, then lift to the sky. "Smoke," he mutters. "Smoke from the shore." Then he is running. Tree limbs dart and reach into him as the earth blurs beneath him. Thunder rolls, shaking the very air around him. Pain sears through his shoulder and the world around him blurs as he falls. His head rocks hard upon the earth. Metal glints in the sunlight and blood pools on moss-covered earth, then his world goes dark.

"Tha bròn orm... I'm sorry." He steps closer. Looking up, Bree sees him clearly for the first time. "Can Ye forgive me?"

Bree's body trembles, her soul thrumming. "You... died." She stares at her past love. "You didn't return because you died."

Slowly Phaisos nods. "I planned to come home to Ye, but I could not. Can Ye forgive me?"

Tears spill down Bree's cheeks. "You wanted to come back to me?"

Phaisos smiles and steps forward, folding his free arm around her. Holding her to him, he kisses her ear. "Oh, yes."

Bree rests her forehead against his shoulder and wraps her arms around him. "I forgive you," she whispers.

With a sigh, the arm around Bree releases. Her past love steps back and looks toward the Sacred Flame. His torch burns brightly above his head.

Her voice is heavy in her throat. "Go in Peace."

He turns his gaze back to her. "And Peace be between us..."

"... now and through all time." They finish the ritual parting together.

With a nod, Phaisos walks to the edge of the blaze. Placing his torch into the fire, he steps into the flames. As the door opens, he pauses, looks back at Bree and smiles. Then he turns and disappears through the doorway.

Her face wet with tears, Bree smiles. "Welcome Home."

Beside her, Britomaris turns to face Bree. "Go raibh mille maith agaibh."

"You are welcome," Bree says through the lump in her throat.

Britomaris walks to the Sacred Flame and glances back at Bree. "Sìochàin doibh." Then she places her torch into the flame, steps into the fire and disappears through the doorway.

Bree stares at the now closing door, tears spilling down her cheeks. "Sìochàin doibh ... Peace be upon ye." Folding her hands over her heart, she murmurs, "Blessed is the Mystery. Sin è."

39

Bree sat at the table in the kitchen of Heather House, her aching head resting in her hands. Eyes closed, she inhaled the peaty aroma wafting from her mug of Glengettie tea. She visualized the soft fragrance washing over the irritated nerves and lulling them to sleep.

So tired.

The storm had raged well into the morning, lashing the house and shaking the windows. Any other night, Bree would have slept through the howling. But, with the crossing of the community of exiles so fresh in her soul, the storm rattled through her as well.

Over and over as the *Bean-Sìdhe* wailed, Bree had relived the same dream...

...A man, raven-haired and painted blue, rises slowly to his feet. Staring into the west, his eyes squint, then lift to the sky. "Smoke," he mutters. "Smoke from the shore." Then he is running. Tree limbs dart and reach into him as the earth blurs beneath him. Thunder rolls, shaking the very air around him. Pain sears through his shoulder and the world around him blurs as he falls. His head rocks hard upon the earth. Metal glints in

the sunlight and blood pools on moss-covered earth, then his world goes dark.

Tears flooded behind her eyelids and spilled slowly down her cheeks. Again and again, she had woken from the dreams weeping. Grief rushing through her, she sobbed herself back into fitful sleep. She cried so much, she had soaked her pillow and had risen to replace it well before sunrise.

She opened her eyes and stared into the golden-brown liquid. *So much sorrow, after so long.*

She could remember it now. She had waited for him. Moon turning upon moon turning, she had waited for Phaisos. Living each day with one eye upon the sea, she willed her love to come home to her. She begged, even pleaded with the waters to carry her love back to their bonfire. But the sea had rolled onto the shore, day after day, empty.

Night upon endless night, she had wondered—what did I do wrong? Why did he never come home?

"Tha bròn orm... I'm sorry." His voice echoed.

She remembered, too, the gentle strength of his arms around her.

A fresh stream of tears dripped down her chin. *At least you know, now. He loved you. He wanted to return, and he loved you.*

Gravel churned in the driveway and Bree shifted her eyes toward the window. The front end of a blue pickup truck popped into view. As the engine fell silent, Bree stood up and walked to the sink. She let the water run cold before splashing her face. She was still drying her hands when Hamish walked into the kitchen.

Hands full of grocery bags, he lifted his chin in greeting. "Hiya. I see ye survived the storm." Setting the bags on the counter, his gaze caught hers and he frowned. He stepped closer, his eyes on her face. He reached for her with his right hand, then let it fall. "Are ye all right?"

His voice wrapped around her, soft and soothing. Bree nodded. "Just tired. I didn't sleep much. The storm."

"Well," he smiled. "At least the inn was kind enough to be

empty for ye this morning." He turned back to the counter and opened one of the bags. "I suppose coffee might hae been a better choice, but..." He pulled out a single, red rose. "For ye."

She stared at the flower. "Hamish..."

He took a step closer to her. "I noticed... ye've only two guests in the inn tomorrow, both arriving early on. Should make it a bit of an easy day. So, I wondered... perhaps ye'd let me cook for ye, tomorrow evening?"

Bree stood considering the man before her. His deep, brown eyes watched her, encouraged her. She wondered how his arms would feel around her and heat prickled under her skin.

"'Tis weeks since ye had a night out." Hamish shifted on his feet, then dropped his gaze to the floor. "Of course, if ye'd rather no..."

She took the rose from his hand. "Dinner sounds lovely."

Lifting his gaze, a smile spread slowly across his face. "Right, then." He stood beaming at her. "Well, I guess I'll be away for now. Until tomorrow."

40

"M'lady." Hamish bowed over his hand. The passenger door of his truck stood open, waiting, with her date, for Bree to enter.

Drawing her shawl more tightly around her shoulders, Bree considered the open door. *Are you sure about this?* She paused, waiting for her soul to answer. As her gaze drifted back to him, she noticed—for the third time this evening—the fine MacLeod hunting tartan shimmying just above his muscular knees.

Hamish's dark eyes peeked up at her. "Have ye forgotten anything?"

"No... no." Bree shook herself into motion. Gathering her ankle-length skirt, she climbed into the truck.

He stood watching her a moment, eyes twinkling in the fading light. Then, with a wink, he closed the door.

Bree's toes tapped nervously inside her boots. *Just breathe.*

She watched him cross in front of the pickup, open the door and settle himself into the driver's seat. Once again Bree noticed the not-quite-formal jacket and button-down shirt beneath the wool scarf around his neck. Even his boots were recently polished. She had to admit—he cleaned up nicely. *But, am I really ready? For this? And with a man?*

The soft, earthy scent of pinesap filled her nose. Turning toward him, Bree stifled a desire to reach out and touch him.

With a quick grin, Hamish started the engine. She saw the muscles in his thighs bunch under his kilt as he engaged the clutch and put the truck into gear. While he steered the pickup onto the A863 toward Dunvegan Village, she noticed his truck was clean, too.

Sunlight glinted over the loch and the Mother Mountain rose into view. Purple heather still spilled down the sloping hillside, but no eyes shimmered for her to see. No bonfires or women danced upon its heights. For once, the mountain was simply a mountain.

Bree smiled. *Welcome Home.*

Glancing in her direction, Hamish caught her smile and offered one in return. Heat flamed across her face and she realized she was blushing. She dropped her chin and let her dark hair fall to conceal her face, then stopped. *You've come this far*, she schooled herself. *Time to see where this goes.*

She tilted her head toward him. "Where is this place?"

Hamish turned back to the road. "Oh, it's no far." Waving at a driver approaching in the other lane, he added, "I hope ye've an appetite, Bree MacLeod."

Bree frowned. "I thought you burned everything in a pan."

"Aye," Hamish nodded, catching her eyes with the corner of his own. "That's right lass, I do."

"Then how can you cook me dinner?"

With a smile, Hamish downshifted, slowing the truck to a stop at the A850 junction. The enormous retaining wall still loomed directly where the road should continue. But tonight, as Bree's gaze tracked the endless rows of stones up to the broad hill towering above her, she saw only the Duirnish Stone.

Hamish steered the truck to the left, following the lochside road toward Dunvegan Castle. As they approached the entrance to the castle grounds, Bree prepared for the truck to turn. But Hamish continued driving.

Bree turned to face him. Catching her puzzled gaze, his eyes twinkled.

"Have ye been out this way? Past the Keep?"

She shook her head. "I haven't even been to the castle."

He glanced at her. "Ach, lass, ye've got to get out more."

When he winked suddenly, Bree had to laugh. *Mischievous laddie, indeed.*

The road narrowed to one lane and curved beneath heavy overgrowth. As Hamish slowed the truck and steered more carefully, they passed a pair of old buildings. Slate tile roofs sloping over low stone walls peeked out of the trees, catching Bree's eye. Gazing at the structures, she marveled. While the windows were missing glass and a few holes needed patching, the stone chimneys were still intact and ready for use.

"A wee bit of tenderness and lovin'—'tis all it needs..." Bree whispered.

The road curved again, and Hamish veered off it and onto a path leading into the woods. Bree gripped the dashboard handle to steady herself as the truck bounced over the rough terrain. *Where is he taking me?*

Hamish steered the truck to the right and Bree gasped. Directly ahead, the woods opened into a grove, a perfect, circular enclosure of trees, beyond which rolled the open sea. Inside the clearing, to her left, a man stood beside a bonfire tending something on an open spit. Small paper lanterns dangled from the lowest limbs of the trees, encircling a table set for two at the very center.

Bree's jaw gaped.

Hamish parked the truck and turned off the ignition. Leaning back in his seat, he turned to face Bree and bowed slightly. "Your table, m'lady."

41

Hamish opened her door and extended his hand to Bree. Gathering her skirt around her, Bree slid out of the truck onto soft earth. *Glad I wore my boots.* The heels she had considered would have made the evening far more uncomfortable.

"Watch yourself." Hamish reached for her hand. Drawing it toward him, he wrapped her arm around his and led her into the clearing. "Tis a wee bit boggy just there."

He was right. The ground pulled at her boots and, steadying herself on his arm, she was glad for the support. With her free hand, she grasped her skirt and drew it up slightly to avoid trailing it in the mushy earth.

Inside the clearing, the ground grew firm under her feet again. With a nod, Hamish released her arm and smiled. "There, now. You're all right." Then he turned and walked toward the man tending the fire. "Hullo, Jock. How goes it?"

Bree watched the two men shake hands. She stared briefly at the unfamiliar face by the fire. *Who is he?* Surely, she must have met him at some point during her interactions in the village. She looked again but still did not recognize him. Then, turning away from the fire, she laughed at herself. *You've only been here eight weeks, after all.* As she chuckled quietly, a breeze drifted through the grove, carrying an aroma that made her mouth water. She had not noticed what was cooking over the fire. Whatever it was, it certainly smelled delicious.

Leaving the men to their conversation, Bree walked closer to the center of the grove. Above her, long limbs stretched and branched from the ancient trees, offering a canopy to the outer half of the clearing. White paper lanterns dotted the tips of those limbs, bathing the stone-top table in soft light—just enough to see comfortably. The table setting shimmered like stars in the paper-lantern moonlight. Blue linen napkins and white ceramic water goblets hugged silver chargers around a glass vase containing three red roses.

She stood blinking back tears as a car engine revved to life behind her. Turning toward the sound, she saw Hamish approaching, his fine MacLeod tartan swaying above his muscular knees. Behind him, Jock's Land Rover disappeared into the woods. She shook her head. "You did all of this? For me?"

Hamish reached out and took her hand in his. Brown eyes locked upon hers, he lifted her hand to his lips and kissed it gently. "I thought it was time we had a proper date."

Bree opened her mouth to speak, but no words came. Closing her mouth, she dropped her gaze. Her hand still rested in his.

"Are ye hungry?"

Bree looked up and nodded. "It smells delicious."

Hamish smiled and drew her toward the table. He pulled out the chair closest to the fire and waited for her to sit. Then he leaned closer to her and pointed to the blaze. "See?"

Bree turned and saw a fish cooking on a spit over the open flame.

"No pan."

Soft and sensual, his breath drifted down Bree's neck. The image of calloused fingers caressing skin flashed through her inner vision and she shivered.

"Are ye cold?"

Bree turned to face him. He was so close. Gentle warmth radiated from his body to spill over hers, while the soft, earthy scent of pinesap filled her nose. She longed to reach out and touch him, to pull him to her. Lips touched in her inner vision and she shivered.

He stood up and gestured over his shoulder. "I've a blanket in the jeep."

Bree stood and shook her head. "No, really, I'm not cold."

Hamish stood there looking at her, his dark eyes shimmering. He took a step closer. "Right, then." Husky and gentle, his voice wrapped tenderly around Bree. "Perhaps a kiss to warm ye?"

Bree's heart raced. *The moment of truth?* Without another thought, she took a step forward and leaned toward him.

"You were happy here." The voice from the Otherworld pounded with her heart in her ears.

His hands glided slowly up her arms and drew her closer to him. Her body shaking, she moved close enough to press against him and froze. *What am I doing?* Inhaling slowly, she closed her eyes and placed her hands upon his chest. "I cannot do this."

Hamish paused and leaned back, opening the space between them.

Bree stood shaking in his arms. Opening her eyes, she lifted her gaze to his. "I'm sorry, Hamish." Gently, she pressed her hands upon his chest and shook her head. "I cannot..."

Taking a step back, his hands slid down her arms to her wrists. "Do ye have someone... in America then?"

She stepped out of his reach. "No," she shook her head. "I did. But not anymore."

He nodded. "Caitlìn mentioned, ye'd lost someone." He tilted his head. "We've no had much time to really talk. But, we do now." He held out his hand to her, palm open and inviting. "Your table awaits, m'lady."

42

Hamish filled her water goblet as Bree stared at her plate.

"Do ye no like salmon?"

Brighid's voice rose out of Bree's memory and flooded through her. *"All beings are sacred and have a place on the circle. Each teaches a unique wisdom, a way of walking with the Sacred. As a Bean feasa, you will work with many Allies to awaken your inner wisdom and to learn to live as Love in every way. You will begin with the five animals of the Celtic Wheel.*

"Salmon guides you through the flow, unveils the wisdom of the emotions and the journey home."

Bree had been a novice when Brighid had introduced her to her circle of Allies. Bear, Eagle, Stag, Salmon, and Raven. She could sense their presence even now, so many years later. She continued to work with them, to learn from them, and needed only to shift her focus briefly to perceive their power coursing through her. These Allies had become closer than friends. They were her family.

It had to be salmon. Bree knew the fish was considered a delicacy, both here and in Seattle. But, in all her years, she had never been able to eat it. Consuming the flesh of one of her Allies —and, in this case, the most ancient of all the animals—seemed like cannibalism. Could she explain it to him? Should she try? After everything else tonight, would he understand?

I really should have asked Caitlin about him.

She lifted her gaze to meet his. *Help me, Salmon. What do I say?*

Hamish's dark eyes grew round. "Have ye an allergy?"

Thank you, Bree whispered mentally as she nodded. "But, the rest is fine. The roasted potatoes, asparagus and spinach salad." She smiled. "They look and smell delicious."

Chuckling, he removed her plate. "Sure, I should hae asked ye." He set the plate of salmon on his charger, then slid the remaining clean plate onto hers. As he settled into his chair, he considered the table. "Ye can have my share of the salad."

Bree smiled. "That's kind of you. But it's really not necessary."

"Aye, lass," he handed her the bowl of spinach salad. "It tis."

She took the bowl. As she dished a helping onto her plate, Hamish spooned potatoes for himself.

He cleared his throat. "So, tell me about your man. Was it long ago that he passed?"

Bree winced. *One year, five months and twelve days.* Placing the salad tongs back into the bowl, she shook her head. "Not long. A little over a year, actually."

Hamish looked up from his plate. "Ach, Bree, I'm so sorry."

"Thanks."

Hamish picked up his fork and started eating. "So, what was he like? How did ye meet?"

Bree took a deep breath. "Actually, it was a she. Her name was Gwen. And she was the love of my life."

Hamish paused, his fork full of salmon halfway to his open mouth. He blinked and set the fork back down on his plate. As he leaned back in his chair, Bree continued.

"She was witty, charming and everyone's best friend. She had a crazy passion for coffee, which she later shared with me, and an endless repertoire of really bad jokes. She owned my favorite café in Saint Louis and, when she smiled at me, I knew everything would be okay."

Bree looked down at her full plate and fidgeted with her fork. *Just breathe.*

"Ye miss her still."

Tears welled in her eyes. Unable to speak through the lump in her throat, she nodded. *This isn't fair. He is so kind. I owe him an explanation.* Her eyes sought his. "But now she is gone. I've been trying to move on, to start again. I just don't know how."

His eyes never left her own. "I could help with that."

"I thought you might, but... it isn't that easy."

He reached across the table and placed his hand over hers. "Would ye like it to be?"

She stared at her hand, still covered by his, and shook her head. "You don't understand. I've never dated a man."

"What, never?"

She looked at him and shook her head. "Never."

He leaned forward. "But, ye agreed to come tonight."

"I did." She gave him a thin smile. "And I still want to be here. But, I realize now, I am just not ready... or able... for more."

"You were happy here." A voice whispered from the Otherworld.

Bree shivered and wrapped her arms around her shoulders. Holding his gaze in her own, she shook her head as a tear spilled down her cheek. "I'm so sorry, truly."

Hamish sat there looking at her, his dark eyes shimmering. Then he stood and walked to her side of the table. Taking her hand in his, he lifted it to his lips and kissed it gently. "If ye should change your mind, I'm your man."

<h1 style="text-align:center">43</h1>

Steam rose from the paper coffee cup nestled in her hands as Bree stared out the window of Inverness Airport. Despite the rain, she had arrived early, only to learn Caitlìn's flight from Gatwick had been delayed while Bree was on the road from Skye. The high-top tables of the arrival hall café were not exactly comfortable, but she preferred them to waiting in the rain.

She looked down at the weak liquid steaming in her cup. *Not exactly Salmon Bay Coffee.* She had emptied her own thermos two hours ago, along the waters of Loch Ness. With another three-hour drive ahead of her, she would need a little more java to get herself and Caitlìn home. *Doesn't even have any foam.* She sighed and took a sip anyway.

Low-hanging clouds glowered at her through the window. The weather seemed to match her mood today. She should be excited to see her kinswoman, and, truth be told, she was. But, with Caitlìn safely returned to Heather House, it would be time for Bree to go home. If only she knew where home was.

She glanced back at the digital display board and searched out Caitlìn's flight number. The word "arrived" blinked on the screen.

Shouldn't be long now. Out of habit, Bree lifted the paper coffee cup. Catching sight of the offensive liquid, she set it back down on the table again. Maybe it would taste better cold.

Fatigue ached along her bones. She shifted on the metal stool and yawned, stretching her back and arms. The past week was still a blur. With Heather House booked to overflowing, Bree had worked late most nights just to finish the chores needed to care for the additional people. Hamish had done his best to help. Friday night, when a guest arrived with several unannounced friends, he squeezed folding cots for the extra guests into the already full room. Where he found them at that late hour, Bree had no idea. The next day, she half expected a call from one of the locals inquiring about missing beds. When no such call came, she wondered if he had conjured them magically.

Settling back on her stool, she chuckled at the thought.

Once again, Hamish had proven to be more than helpful. He drove to Portree for groceries, ran the extra loads of laundry, even changed a flat tire for a rather distressed guest. Saturday night, utterly exhausted, Bree fell asleep, head resting in her arms on the kitchen counter. Hamish had draped a blanket over her shoulders and left an alarm to wake her Sunday morning in time to prepare breakfast for the night's guests.

Gazing out the window, Bree sighed. It was just as well she chose not to start up a relationship with Hamish, she told herself for the umpteenth time. Heather House was really all she could manage right now.

She frowned. Had she really made the right choice? Hamish had been nothing but kind and caring, even before that night in the grove. He had been so gentle throughout their date, despite her fumblings. She could still see the soft glow of his eyes as he had kissed her hand goodnight. Since then, they had worked together day after day and he never pressed her, not in the slightest. His words, his gestures, even his banter offered friendly tenderness. But, every time she looked into his eyes, she knew—he longed to try again.

What about me? What do I long for?

Raindrops spattered a fine sheen upon the windows in front of her. Bree sighed. *If only I knew.*

"Is that for me?"

Bree shifted in her seat to find Caitlìn standing next to her. Her kinswoman reached across the table and grabbed the cup of coffee. Bree opened her mouth to speak, to warn her friend not to drink the disgusting liquid, but Caitlìn was already gulping it. Bree chuckled. "You bet."

Caitlìn emptied the contents and placed the paper cup back on the table. Scanning the empty surface, she frowned. "What?" She stared at Bree. "No scone?"

Bree laughed. Sliding off the metal stool, she pulled her kinswoman into a hug. "Fáilte abhaile, mo chara... Welcome home."

44

Bree walked along the edge of the cliff, letting her gaze drift across the waters of the Sound of Raasay. With Caitlìn home and back to caretaking Heather House, she found the free time she had been missing since her arrival on Skye. Over the past week since her kinswoman's return, Bree had remained close to the B&B, often helping with the endless chores. But today, she opted to explore the island.

Ahead of her, the rugged, basalt rock face stretched as far as she could see. She paused to consider the odd, folded formations and remembered the locals called these cliffs Kilt Rock. "For they look ever so like the swaying folds of a man's kilt as he walks." As she said it, Caitlìn had waggled her eyebrows and nodded toward Hamish as he walked out of the kitchen, away from them.

Does she know? Bree still wondered. Certainly she had not mentioned her short-lived flirtation with the man. Had he?

Bree sighed. *Why did I push him away?* She had to admit, they shared an attraction. But she walked away. Why?

She dropped her gaze to the ground beneath her and shook her head. She had replayed their encounter in the grove so many times since that night. She still found herself believing it could have ended differently. *Maybe I could try again?*

She shivered.

Drawing her fleece jacket closed against the cool breeze, Bree lifted her gaze and admired the rolling green hills of Raasay Island. According to the guidebook she had read, no one lived there anymore. The water table became tainted with salt water from the Sound of Raasay, leaving no fresh water for people to drink. So they left, abandoning their homes and the isle. The thought filled her with sorrow.

"Beautiful, is she no?"

Bree furrowed her brow and turned toward the voice. A man stood to her left. His copper-colored hair flowed down the sides of his weathered face as painted lines spiraled down his cheek, shoulder and arm. Tall and muscular, the sunlight drifted through him, adding to his Otherworldly appearance. Watching his kilt sway in the breeze, Bree wondered where she had seen him before.

"I always loved her." Rocking onto his heels, the man smiled broadly, then turned to Bree. His face falling to neutral, he cleared his throat. "The isle, that is."

Bree blinked. She tried to reply, but she could only stare.

The ghostly man laughed. "Nothing quite like it. After endless moons staring at the open sea, tae catch a glimpse of her and know—you're home." He nodded. "Then tae feel your feet upon her, warm and welcoming. Ach, 'tis no greater pleasure." He looked at Bree. "Do Ye no agree?"

Bree shook her head. "I wouldn't know."

The man stood considering her, then placed his hands upon his hips. "Tis a sorrow, that is, for certain." Then his eyes twinkled and he leaned closer to Bree. "Ach now, would Ye *like* to know?"

Bree gazed out across the waters. "I suppose. But that would require knowing where home is."

"Aye, that it would." The man's voice drifted to her with the breeze. Watching the waves roll onto the Raasay shore, Bree shivered into her fleece jacket. "Perhaps she can help Ye sort that."

Bree furrowed her brow and turned back toward the man. Fierce green eyes met her gaze instead.

Long, black hair cascaded unbound down the woman's back as

blue ink spiraled down the left side of her face and throat and disappeared under the familiar plaid. Bree smiled and the woman bowed her head. "Tis time I thank Ye, Child of the Sìdhe, for helping me and mine. Tae give Ye a gift in return."

Bree shook her head. "That isn't necessary."

The woman stepped closer. "Aye, it tis." Raising her left hand, the woman pressed her palm to Bree's forehead.

Light blazed through Bree. Brilliant and stark, it seared across her forehead, blinding her. Gasping, she closed her eyes against the glare. Sliding from the inner corner of her left eyebrow to the right, the white light arched downward, passed just above the bridge of her nose, and curved back upward to hover above the inner corner of her right eyebrow. With a flash, it arched slowly downward again, this time passing well above the bridge of her nose as it seared a line on its way back to her left eyebrow. The outline complete, the image of a crescent flamed again through Bree's inner vision.

Blinking furiously, Bree bent over and leaned her hands upon her knees. As her vision cleared, a trail of light streamed before her. Curving away from the cliffs, it led deeper into the hills of Skye.

Bree took three steps to follow the trail, then hesitated. Her mind whispered caution, but her soul screamed, *Go!* Caught between the two, Bree stood shivering. To her surprise, she realized she longed to follow the trail of light to its source.

The ghostly man beside her chuckled. "On Ye go. He's waiting for Ye."

45

Bree's breath came hard and fast. She had been climbing these rolling hills for almost an hour. Still, the trail of light blazed before her, called her onward.

"Crrruck!"

Bree paused and looked up into a brilliant, blue sky. A single dark spot spiraled overhead. Panting slightly, she smiled. Raven had sent one of her own to guard her. She touched her brow. "Blessed is the Mystery."

The trail of light wound up and around the knoll ahead of her. "C'mon girl," she prompted herself and started climbing. The path was steep and she dug her hands into the earth to steady herself. As she cleared the rise, the earth sloped downward and she stopped short. A wall of enormous, round stones rose out of the mound in front of her. Buried in earth, they looked to her like a doorway, but to what?

Her eyes tracked the stones. Following their curves up to the broad hillock crest towering above her, she spotted an old, broken flat of wood compressed between the stones below and the earth above them. Frowning slightly, she leaned closer. Were those hash marks etched into the wood? Or were they just the etchings of time?

Light flashed, tracing the marks. Unable to resist, Bree reached out and skimmed her fingers across the etchings. Silvery-white light blazed through her inner vision, blanching her world. As the brilliance swallowed her, Bree closed her eyes and slipped through the whiteness into the Otherworld.

46

Feet bare upon cold earth, Bree stands shivering. A wall of enormous stones rises above her. Covered in freshly-turned earth, the mound aches like an open wound.

Cold.

Her hands throb and Bree lifts them closer. Blisters pucker through black soil that seeps into endless open cuts and gashes. Blinking back tears, she stares at the blood oozing through the dark stains. Blood. Her blood.

She turns her hands over and over, searching for an uninjured spot but finding none. "I don't understand."

"Don't you remember?" Bear stands beside her. Her Ally nods toward the wall of stones. "You built this tomb."

"Tomb?"

Bree shifts her gaze back to the wall of stones. White light blazes and swirls before her. Her arms grow heavy and she struggles to hold the weight building in her hands. Her knees buckle and she crumples to the ground. Her head rocks toward the earth and hits something hard. Rubbing her forehead, she pushes herself to kneeling with her free hand. Long, black hair slips over her left shoulder and spills in front of her. As she pushes it to her back, she gasps. A man lies dead on the ground in front of her, his red hair spilling down his side like blood.

"Can you remember, mo Ghrá... my Love?" Bríghid's voice echoes around her. "Can you remember the heart you loved more than your own?"

Bree lowers a shaking hand onto the red-haired man's chest. An embroidered sleeve spills down her arm. Her eyes trace the spirals, stitched to honor her acceptance into the Mystery.

"I could not save him." Her voice trembles as tears slip down her cheeks. "All my knowledge, all my training and I could not save him."

Warmth spreads through her shoulder. "You were not meant to, Bree Nic Bhríde."

Turning her head to the left, Bree stares into the loving gaze of Mother Bríghid. The hand of the goddess rests upon Bree's shoulder.

"My name..." A sob builds in Bree's throat. "I gave up my name for his. For the love of a man, I went against chief and clan. I lost my people, my place of belonging." Her gaze again seeks the man before her. "And he died." Her voice cracks. "He died and his people refused me. They held me responsible, declared me outcast... exiled..." Her body shivers as the sob wrenches its way up and out, spilling a cascade of tears. "For the love of a man, I lost it all."

"Tha bròn orm..." The voice of her former lover echoes around her. "...I'm sorry."

And Bree remembers. Those were his parting words. As she fought for his life, he breathed those words, then nothing more.

Bree's body shakes. She rocks, each trembling sway of her body summoning another watershed. As the tears flood down her cheeks, she slumps forward and rests her head upon his chest. Through the tears, she sees it again... his lifeless body sprawled upon the floor... her shaking hands trying to revive him... her body bent over his, pressed to his, in search of warmth but finding only cold.

Closing her eyes, Bree moans. Two men. Phaisos and her red-haired lover. Both left her, never to return. And for the second man, she sacrificed everything. Wave upon wave of forgotten sorrow pounds through her. Surrendering to the onslaught, she wails. Her sides ache with each pull and she collapses into the tide and lets it empty her.

Cold. She shivers.

Warmth trickles into her, spilling slowly from the center of her back.

She lifts her head and peers through strands of black hair to see Bríghid's arm disappearing behind her.

"Mo Ghrá... my Love, what did you do then?"

"I buried him." She presses herself up to kneeling and looks at the tomb before her. "I carried him here and buried him. I dug the earth and moved the stones with my own two hands."

"And then?" Bear's gentle voice washes over her.

Bree blinks back tears, her voice trembling with her body. "I exiled myself. I forfeited my name for his, that I should always remember. And I banished myself, never to love another man and to wander in exile."

She could remember now. She sees herself, chemise stained and torn, pulling loose the braid in her hair that declared her mated. Blood smeared on her face, black hair streaming down her back, she walks into the darkness. Only the stones and the earth remain.

"And what was his name?"

Shaking, Bree stares into the eyes of Mother Bríghid.

"Mo Ghrá... my Love, what was the name you chose to mark your exile?"

Bree's lips tremble. Tears pooling in her eyes, her voice is a whisper. "MacLeod."

Bríghid nods as a sob catches in Bree's throat.

"You have wandered long enough." The goddess smiles, releasing rays of light to stream around Bree. "But only you can end your exile. You imposed it. Now you must end it."

Bree shakes her head. "How?"

"Put it down."

Her arms grow heavy and she struggles to hold the weight building in her hands. Shifting her gaze, Bree discovers she carries an enormous stone, etched like the wooden lintel of the tomb.

"Put it down," Bear reaffirms Bríghid's guidance.

Tears spill down Bree's cheeks. "How?"

"Crrruck!" Midnight-black wings stretch and spiral above her, as her Raven Ally descends and settles upon the top of the mound. Just below her Ally, Bree sees a hole in the wall of stones.

Bree nods and rises, shaking, to her feet. With the hem of her chemise trailing upon the earth behind her, Bree carries the stone to the tomb and presses it into the wall. As her hands withdraw from the stone's surface, both her lover and her sorrow are gone.

She steps back from the wall and the tomb disappears into the earth before her.

"Now what?" Her voice is a whisper.

Bear nudges Bree's hand with her snout. Something solid presses into Bree's palm and she lifts her hand to examine it. A stone carving of a fleur-de-lys rests in the palm of her hand.

Brighid smiles. "Time to go home, Bree Nic Bhríde."

47

Late-afternoon sunlight streamed through the broad, bay window of Heather House, bathing Bree and the room in golden warmth. Hands resting in the back pockets of her jeans, she let her gaze drift across the waters of the loch.

The voice of Caitlìn's mother whispered through her. *"Go now, if ye can, before the song of Skye thrums in your veins. For the Isle will claim ye and ye'll never want to leave. Skye never lets go of Her own."*

Bree sighed. Sure, the isle had claimed her long ago. But, was she really one of Skye's own? Her journey yesterday revealed Skye to be a place of exile for Bree, a place of loss where she had surrendered even her name. While she was certain she could live here, would it ever truly be home?

"That's the last of it." Caitlìn carried the basket of freshly dried sheets into the room and placed it on the coffee table. Looking at the heaping pile, she shook her head. "I'd forgotten the endless loads of laundry." Bree turned to face Caitlìn and her friend smiled. "Bet ye did nay know how many ye could do in a day."

Bree chuckled. "I do now."

Caitlìn pulled a flat sheet from the basket and started folding. As her friend's hands reacquainted themselves with the familiar process, a gentle shimmering flowed across her friend's shoulders.

Bree smiled. The mantle of power was clearly restored to the rightful guardian of Heather House.

So, now what?

"Here," Bree called. "Let me help you." Sliding her hands out of her pockets, Bree walked over to the table, reached into the basket and grabbed a sheet.

Caitlìn leaned over and placed her folded sheet on the overstuffed sofa. She straightened back to standing and paused, her gaze drifting through the window. "I've missed this view." Her friends's voice was deep, almost husky. Bree's throat ached from her friend's unshed tears. Caitlìn cleared her throat. "I'm not sure I could leave it again."

"I know." Bree folded the sheet over her arm. "I will miss it, too."

Caitlìn turned to face her. "You're leaving."

Bree nodded. "It's time I was heading home."

"Back to Ireland, then?"

Bree placed the folded sheet on the overstuffed sofa and shook her head. As she turned back toward the basket, she found Caitlìn staring at her.

"You're no going back to St. Louis?"

Bree sighed. "I have to."

Caitlìn stepped close enough to Bree to grasp her hands. "Why do ye have to? If it's Gwen ye feel ye owe..."

"No." Bree shook her head. "It's not that."

Caitlìn furrowed her brow. "What, then?"

"I left my life there." Bree's eyes caught those of her kinswoman. "I just left it. Tossed to the wind and scattered in a hundred pieces." Bree shrugged. "Whether it will remain there or not, I cannot quite say. But I won't know until I go back, pick up the pieces and start living again."

Caitlìn held Bree's gaze. "Are ye sure?"

Bree wished she could say no. But the image of the fleur-de-lys gifted at the end of her journey yesterday flooded back to her, erasing any doubts. She knew all too well, amongst its other historical references, the fleur-de-lys was the symbol of the city of

St. Louis. Her Allies were showing her the way forward, just as she had asked.

Blinking back tears, Bree nodded.

Her kinswoman sighed. "Right, then." Caitlìn squeezed her hands and let them go. "Know this—ye have a place here any time ye have need or want of it. And, in the meantime, remember what my mother said."

"Your mother?"

Her kinswoman smiled. "'A wee bit of tenderness and lovin'—'tis all it needs...'" Caitlìn drew Bree into a hug. "Be gentle with yourself, okay?"

Sunlight glinted off the water of the loch. For a moment, for one beat of her heart, green eyes shimmered in the light. "I promise," Bree whispered.

48

Eyes closed, Bree pressed her forehead against the rough surface of the Duirnish Stone. A gentle hum rose from the ancient monolith and she breathed in the greeting. Letting her hands slide to the sides of the stone, she touched her lips to its surface.

"*Go raibh mille maith agaibh...* Thank you, Ancient One."

Her breath flowed warm upon the stone and her hands tingled in response. As the hum deepened, she knew the stone had heard her.

She stepped back and opened her eyes. Reaching into the pocket of her favorite black fleece jacket, she pulled out a silver flask about the size of her palm. Three dragons spiraled across the flask's surface, their tails disappearing into endless, interlocking curls. Bree unscrewed the top and breathed in the peaty fragrance. "*Uisce beatha...* The Waters of Life." With a brief smile, she raised the flask up before her and emptied a pour of whiskey onto the land between her and the stone.

"Blessed is the Mystery."

The wind gusted, pulling at her scarf and sending her hair dancing across her cheeks and forehead. Smiling, she turned her face into the wind. As the black strands of her hair shifted to stream behind her, she let her gaze drift over Dunvegan valley.

"Time to go home, Raven Child." The voice of the Old Man breathed through her.

Sunlight glinted off the waters of the loch and Bree closed her eyes against the glare. Etched on her inner vision was the flowing image of a fleur-de-lys.

Bree smiled. "Thank you, Ancient One." She bowed knowing the Old Man would see her.

Opening her eyes, Bree let her gaze drift once more across this view of Dunvegan Valley. She wanted to remember it all. The loch, the heather, the Mother Mountain. She suspected, in the days and months to come, she would remember this place and wonder.

She lifted her fingers to her forehead and bowed to the valley. Then, she turned and walked down Dunvegan tor.

So, Brighid was right. MacLeod is not my true name after all. Would it be the same, marching in the annual parade of clans? Could she still wear the green and purple hunting plaid of the MacLeods of Skye and know she belonged? In her mind's eye she could see the part of her who had argued with Mother Brighid only a few weeks earlier. She gazed into the eyes of her soul and sighed. *We have to give it up, you know.*

Her soul stared back at her. *Why? Who is Bree Nic Bhríde anyway?*

Bree tilted her head. *I don't know. But, I believe it is time we found out. Wouldn't you agree?*

Her soul stared. Then she closed her eyes, turned and walked away.

Black hair dancing in the wind, her gaze tracking the land beneath her, Bree worked her way down the hill. "Bree Nic Bhríde," she whispered, letting the name wash over her.

Heat flamed through her cheeks and she lifted her gaze. In the pullout just below her, a blue pickup truck was parked next to her Citroën. While she could not see the face of the kilted man leaning against the truck, one foot tucked underneath him, the familiar sweater confirmed her inner knowing.

That green deepens the brown of his eyes. Bree sighed. *You had your chance. Time to let that one go, too.*

Bree climbed the rest of the way down the hill and stepped

onto the gravel of the pullout. As the stones rustled under her feet, Hamish glanced up at her.

"I saw your car." He shrugged, pushing himself off the bumper. "The last time it was parked here... Well..." He stepped closer to her. "I wanted to be certain ye were all right."

Bree offered him a thin smile. "I'm all right. Thanks."

He nodded toward the tor. "Out hillwalking again?"

She chuckled softly. "Not exactly."

The soft, earthy scent of pinesap filled her nose and she took a step closer. *No*, Bree schooled herself, stifling the desire to reach out and touch him. *You've got to tell him. Now.* His dark eyes watched her, calm and serious. She took a breath to speak, then looked at the ground instead. *Mother Bríghid, help me.*

"You're going back, to America. Are ye no?"

Unable to speak through the lump in her throat, she just nodded.

He dropped his gaze to the ground. Rocking back onto his heels, he shifted his hands to his hips before finding her eyes. "Well, I cannae follow ye there."

She turned her face to him, tears filling her eyes. "No." She cleared her throat. "But, it is kind of you to make me believe you would want to."

He took a step closer. Drawing her hand into his, he lifted it to his lips and kissed it gently. "Should ye, one day, find yourself opening an inn of your own," his eyes held hers, "I'm your man."

With a soft squeeze, he released her hand and stepped back toward the truck.

"Hamish."

"No." He shook his head. "No goodbyes, lass. Only good wishes."

His eyes lingered on her a while, then he turned and walked back to his truck. A tear slid down Bree's cheek as she watched him open the door and settle himself into the driver's seat. He started the engine and put the truck into gear. Then, with a half wave, he steered the truck back onto the A850.

Bree stood watching the blue truck until it disappeared in the distance. "Trust." She hugged herself. "I choose to trust in Love."

She opened the right-side door to the Citroën and settled herself in the driver's seat. Her purse rested on the passenger seat, half-open. Reaching in, she pulled out her telephone and tapped the screen until she found the number she wanted. Pressing dial, she lifted the telephone to her ear.

Should have known I would get his voicemail.

She waited through the familiar recording before speaking. "Hey Fergus, it's Bree. I'm coming home."

EPILOGUE

"Bree!" A woman squealed from behind the espresso machine, then launched herself over the counter. Arms flailing over red hair, she ran at the newcomer. "Bree! Breeeeeee!"

"Hello, Sheila." Bree gestured to the woman as the door to Café de Lys closed behind her. She took three steps into the space and stopped. Sunlight streamed through the floor-to-ceiling windows, flooding the café and bathing the guests sitting on the overstuffed sofas in soft, golden light. Faery light, Gwen used to call it, her own kiss of magic.

Bree looked around the open room and sighed. *I'm really here.*

"Bree!"

"Ooooooof!" Bree turned toward Sheila's voice and found herself lifted into a bear hug. Her toes just reaching the floor, she struggled to keep her balance.

As Bree's feet settled onto wood again, Sheila stepped back and propped her hands on her hips. "Fergus said you'd be coming." She chuckled and shook her head. "Serves me right for not believing him. I thought he was teasing me, again."

"She's so quick to laugh, that one." Gwen's voice echoed through Bree. Dropping her gaze to the left, a ghostly image of her former lover flickered in the sunlight, standing beside her. Just like she

always did. The ghostly woman smiled at Bree. *"And she's so easy to tease."*

Bree blinked back tears as a gentle warmth spread up her legs and torso.

"You look well enough." Sheila's gaze softened, bathing Bree in tender compassion. "Glad you're back with us."

Bree lifted her eyes to meet the woman's and offered her a thin smile. *Am I?*

Red eyebrows darted upward. "The usual?"

"Sure." Bree nodded. "Why not?"

"Right!" Sheila clapped her hands together and rubbed them. "Coming right up!"

Bree watched Gwen's favorite barista stride back toward the coffee bar. *She and Gwen, they always loved this place.* Bree sighed and looked around the room. Soft, golden sunlight spilled from the windows, illuminating her favorite loveseat. She walked up to the overstuffed chair, reached out and ran her fingers along the ribbing on the lavender throw pillows.

"You must help me."

Bree lifted her gaze toward the woman's voice. Oak trees stretched all around her, their autumn leaves spilling a sea of orange and red through the old-growth forest. Her breath clouded before her, lingering on the damp, chilly air, and she shivered. She turned to look for the woman who had summoned her here.

"You must help me."

Turning toward the frantic voice, Bree hit something solid. Fire seared across her arm.

"Oh, Bree!" Sheila cried out and took a step back. "I'm so sorry!"

A cloth napkin pressed against her arm as Sheila cleaned the spilled coffee from her skin. In Bree's inner vision, blood seeped from the red cloth and dripped onto the floor at her feet.

"Are you okay?"

Bree lifted her gaze. Before her, a ceramic chalice curved in Sheila's hands. Etched in spiraling chevrons, the ancient vessel radiated opalescent light.

"Bree?"

Sheila touched her arm and Bree's gaze snapped to meet the woman's. When she looked back at Sheila's hands, they held an ordinary cup of coffee. Bree frowned.

"Here," Sheila's voice flowed soft, encouraging Bree into the overstuffed chair. "Have a seat. Just relax and let me care for you for a while."

GLOSSARY
IRISH AND SCOTS GAELIC PHRASES AND PRONUNCIATION

The sounds of the English language differ from those of the Irish and Scots Gaelic. The pronunciations listed here are attempts at phonetic renderings of Gaelic sounds. Please know that these are approximations only, a starting point for those daring enough to try.

A stór... dearest, my dear, darling. Used to refer to a cherished family member or loved one. Pronounced "uh store."

Ach... Both Irish and Scots Gaelic, literally "But" or "Well". Prounced "ach" with the ch aspirated in the throat (like the word "loch").

Aes Dána... the Gifted, those blessed by the goddess Dánu / Dána and imbued with Otherworldly skills. Pronounced "ace donna."

Airds... the directions of the Celtic Wheel: north, east, south, west and center. Pronounced like "arts" but with "air" in place of "ar"... "air-ts."

Alba... in Irish and Scots Gaelic, this is the word for Scotland. Pronounced "all-buh."

Anam cara... soul friends. Pronounced "on-um car-uh."

Bean Feasa... wise woman, druid, walker between the worlds. Pronounced "bahn fah-sah."

Beannachtaí... blessings. Pronounced "bahn-nach-tee," with the "nach" aspirated in the throat.

Beannachtaí, a stór... Blessings, dearest. Pronounced "bahn-nach-tee a store."

Beannachtaí, mo Ghrá... Blessings, my love. Pronounced "bahn-nach-tee moe hraw."

Bean-Sìdhe... A woman of the Ancient Ones, a banshee. Pronounced "Bahn-she."

Bha thusa ceàrr, a mhàthair... Scots Gaelic for "You were wrong, mother." Pronounced "Wuh too-suh key-are uh wah-hair."

Bree Nic Bhríde... Bree MacLeod's Gaelic name, literally meaning Bree daughter of Bríde. Pronounced "bree nick vree-je."

Bríde... a variation of the name Bríghid. Pronounced "bree-je."

Brígh... a variation of the name Bríghid. Pronounced "bree-he," with the "he" as a slight aspiration in the throat at the end.

Bríghid... the Celtic goddess of the forge, smithcraft, poetry, midwifing and the keeper of the Sacred Flame. Pronounced "bree-hid" or "bree-git."

Caitlin... Irish and Scottish woman's name, a version of Kathleen. Pronounced "kuh-shleen."

Chiya... although not actually Irish, the word deserves explanation. First encountered in Marion Zimmer Bradley's *Darkover* series, the term has stayed in my vocabulary. The closest translation is *dearest, dear heart* or *beloved*. Pronounced "chee-yuh" or "shee-yuh."

Clooties... strips of cloth or ribbon tied to sacred trees in a Celtic act of prayer. Like prayer ties, they are left on special trees to carry the prayer to the Sacred through the elements. (Also spelled *clooties*.)

Deiseal...Irish for sunwise or clockwise movement. To turn *deiseal* is to invoke the positive, constructive flow of creation. Pronounced "Jay-shull."

an Drochaid an Eilein Sgitheanaich... Scots Gaelic for The Skye Bridge. Pronounced "on droe-hood on eye-lynn ski-on-ach."

Éireann... Ireland. Also the name of one of the three mother goddesses of Ireland. Pronounced "erin."

Fáilte abhaile... Welcome home. Pronounced "fall-chuh a-wall-ye."

Fáth Fíth... an incantation chanted to cast a cloak of invisibility upon someone. Pronounced "faw fee."

Fiona... an Irish girl's name, meaning "Bright" or "Fair one". Pronounced "fee-oh-na."

Fomorian... A primordial being of decomposition, decay and entropy in the Celtic mystical tradition.

Go raibh mille maith agaibh... Thank you (formal). Pronounced "go rev meal-uh my uh-give."

Is deas bualadh leat... Lovely to meet you. Pronounced "iss jass bull-uh lot."

Imbas... The light of illumination and inspiration that flows at the heart of all creation and creative activity. Pronounced like the English word "emboss," only with equal stress upon both syllables, "im-boss."

Machair... the soil, the earth of Ireland. Pronounced "ma-hair."

Màire... a woman's name in Scots Gaelic, the equivalent of Mary or Maureen in English. Pronounced "maw-ruh."

Mo Ghrá... my love. Pronounced "moe hraw."

Mo ghràidh... Scots for "My love." Pronounced "moe hraw."

Pàiste an Shìdhe... Scots for "Child of the People of Peace." Pronounced "paw-sh-tuh on ee-yuh."

Sasannach... in both Irish and Scots Gaelic, literally "Englishman" or "person from England." Colloquially used to mean interloper, intruder or one who does not belong. Pronounced "suh-sen-ach."

Scotia... The Mother Goddess of Scotland, after whom Scotland and Nova Scotia are named. Pronounced "skoh-shuh."

Sgian dubh... Scots Gaelic, the name of a small, single-edged knife traditionally kept concealed in the legging or boot. Pronounced "skee-un doov."

the Sídhe... also called the People of Peace and the Ancient Ones. The *Sídhe* are the ancient guardians of and the in dwelling spirits of the land. *Sídhe* is pronounced "she."

Sin é... literally, "It is". Used as the equivalent of "Amen" or "So mote it be". Pronounced "shin-a," with the "a" sounding long, as in "hay," but without the "h" sound.

Síocháin duit... Irish for "Peace be upon you." Pronounced "she-uh-hawn doot."

Tapadh leat... Scots for "Thank you." Used for single individual. Pronounced "tuh-pug lot."

Tapadh libh... Also Scots for "Thank you." Used for multiple people or when speaking respectfully. Pronounced "tuh-pug live."

Thà bròn orm... Scots for "I am sorry." Pronounced "haw brone or-um."

Thà fàilte romhat... Scots for "You are welcome." Pronounced "haw fall-chuh row-ut."

Uisce beatha... literally, "Waters of life." The Irish word for whiskey. Pronounced "ish-kuh bay-huh."

REFERENCES & RESOURCES

For those curious souls who would like to know more about the Otherworld, Celtic mysticism, Druidry, and the shamanic universe, here are some doorways:

Carmina Gadelica. Carmichael, Alexander. Lindisfarne Press, 1992.

The Celtic Book of the Dead. Matthews, Caitlín. St. Martin's Press, 1992.

Celtic Myths and Legends. Berresford Ellis, Peter. Running Press, 1999.

The Celtic Shaman. Matthews, John. Element Books Limited, 1991.

Dreamtime and Inner Space. Kalweit, Holger. Shambhala Publications, Inc., 1984.

The Druid Animal Oracle. Carr-Gomm, Philip and Stephanie. Simon & Schuster, 1994.

Druid Mysteries. Carr-Gomm, Philip. Rider, 2002.

The Encyclopedia of Celtic Wisdom. Matthews, Caitlín and John. Element Books Limited, 1994.

Fire in the Head. Cowan, Tom. Harper San Francisco, 1993.

From the Cauldron Born. Hughes, Kristoffer. Llewellyn Publications, 2012.

The Journey into Spirit. Hughes, Kristoffer. Llewellyn Publications, 2014.

Living Druidry. Restall Orr, Emma. Piatkus, 2004.

Mother of the Isles. Smith, Jill. Dor Dama Press, 2003.

Rekindling the Flame: A Pilgrimage in the Footsteps of Brigid of Kildare. Minehan, Rita. Solas Bhríde Community, 1999.

The Sacred World of the Celts. Pennick, Nigel. Inner Traditions International, 1997.

Shamanism. Eliade, Mircea. Princeton University Press, 1964.

Shamanism As a Spiritual Practice. Cowan, Tom. The Crossing Press, 1996.

The Sídhe. Matthews, John. The Lorian Association, 2004.

Singing the Soul Back Home. Matthews, Caitlín. Element Books Limited, 1995.

The Way of the Shaman. Harner, Michael. Harper San Francisco, 1980.

ACKNOWLEDGMENTS

ABOUT THE AUTHOR

Jennifer Lynn is a soul midwife, a shamanic Druid Priestess, and a modern-day mystic specializing in Celtic mystical techniques and practices. During thirty years of training and experience, she has studied extensively with Tom Cowan, Caitlín Matthews, Geo Cameron, Hank Wesselman, the Invisible Druid Order, the Order of Bards Ovates and Druids, the Foundation for Shamanic Studies as well as with mystical practitioners internationally.

Jennifer gives voice to her Bardic craft through poetry and prose. She is the author of the award-winning, mystical fiction series Bree MacLeod's Story (*Being Here, Coming Home* and *The Chalice and the Blade*). Her writings explore the rhythms of life while honoring the Goddess and the Sacred Conversation.

Jennifer is also a Chinese medicine practitioner and a Minister of the Circle of the Sacred Earth, a church of animism fostering shamanic principles and practices.

For more about Jennifer Lynn and to follow Bree MacLeod's Story, visit:

www.ThroughShamansEyes.wordpress.com
www.youtube.com/@throughshamanseyes
www.patreon.com/TheMysticsCircle

ALSO BY JENNIFER LYNN

Being Here, book one of Bree MacLeod's Story

The Chalice and the Blade , book three of

Bree MacLeod's Story

Coming soon... book four of Bree MacLeod's Story

www.ingramcontent.com/pod-product-compliance
Lightning Source LLC
Chambersburg PA
CBHW031529310726
48971CB00008B/2410